Indelible Island

Indelible Island

Iridescent Toad Publishing

Iridescent Toad Publishing.

Cover art by Eerilyfair Design.

First edition. ISBN: 978-1-9163478-6-1

Extra special thanks to Tanya Lee Clark for helping me bring this book to life.

Chapter One

K ate enjoyed the calmly moving country through which they had been travelling. The gritty concrete road curved away from the tall, overbearing evergreen trees. The narrow shadows created a red glow from the woods, yet the sky remained clear.

It was all unfamiliar to Kate. It was nothing like the town. Nothing like where she was from. She told herself that she didn't need to be anxious; it was surely inevitable that a woman beginning a new life in a new place would be somewhat daunted by such a drastic change of scenery. And yet, in her mind's eye, Kate kept seeing the quiet little hillside near her childhood home, the familiar townspeople and the usual reliable humdrum of the familiar. She tried to snap herself out of her reverie as she reminded herself that she needed to focus on the now, on the present.

Suddenly, the road became less bumpy and she could see a steeple in the distance. It stood proudly as if to function as a landmark for a change in the texture of the road as their car continued to cruise along at a continuous speed. The road curved again, and she could feel the pressure of the wind against the side of the vehicle. They passed a row of houses, then another, and then another. Surely, they were at their destination by now? She could hear what she thought were seagulls in the distance.

"I think I'll like it here," she said cheerfully, turning to face her new husband.

Ford was listening but it would have been easy for Kate to perceive that he wasn't. His blue eyes didn't glance at her and his ashy coloured face didn't turn to acknowledge her reassuringly.

"We're not there yet, Kate. This is only Springfield," he replied to her, half-heartedly attentive.

It was only for a short while that Kate managed to conceal her nervousness. Her need for more information soon overwhelmed her.

"It will be ok? Won't it?" she asked quietly.

"I don't see why it wouldn't be, Kate."

She felt so damn tense. Kate needed it to be ok. It had to be ok. She had left behind everything she had ever known due to having fallen for Ford in a whirlwind romance. The immediate love she felt for him was such that it was a choice of either moving thousands of miles to begin her life with him or wondering about what she may have missed. She didn't want to suffer the eternity of the heartache, so here she was, sat in his car, married to him and wondering what her new home would be like.

Kate had always doubted her ability to make good decisions. She looked at Ford and she wondered, was he concentrating intensively on the driving or had his charm worn off. Surely, she was just upsetting herself and being irrational and paranoid due to what was the inevitable nervousness of having made such a commitment.

As if having read her thoughts, Ford gently put his warm hand on her thigh.

"Kate, everything is going to be fine. This is going to be a new and beautiful chapter and we are going to have a good life together."

Kate nodded and felt loved from feeling his touch as she repeated, "a good life together."

"Remember Kate, you don't know the island," Ford stated firmly. "Don't judge it until you have seen it for yourself. Just take things one day at a time, then you'll be fine."

His words glided over her as she turned her head to look at the sea out of the window. It glistened prettily.

"You mustn't be afraid if it takes you some time to get used to your new home," Ford continued. "Or indeed, if it takes you some time to get used to living with me."

"You won't be different, don't be silly," Kate replied, slightly irritated.

It was then that Ford grinned and suddenly he was the cheeky, exuberant man who had saved her from how lonely she was before she had met him. He was a fun person to be with and he was her friend. She knew that. It had to be true.

Kate took in a long deep breath and enjoyed his scent. His hair was slightly messy with the beginnings of a widow's peak and his face was firm; a stern expression on high cheekbones with a thin, yet expressive, mouth.

In the time that Kate had spent taking in his appearance once again, she became so worried that maybe Ford was going cold on her.

"Is it going to turn out that you're one of those women with too many questions?" Ford asked her frankly. "I should hope not, Kate."

"I guess I just need to know that this is all going to be ok," sighed Kate.

Ford drummed his long fingers against the firmness of the steering wheel. His eyes narrowed to focus on the road, more so than the shape of the road really demanded. He seemed irritated somehow. Kate bowed her head and looked down into her lap at the pattern on the hem of her dress. The nights would be drawing in soon. Autumn was well on the way. She wondered if by the time it was winter, she would still feel as reassured by the man that she had chosen to spend the rest of her life with. It all seemed so simple when she had made the decision at the time.

They came to a car park and Ford swiftly found a spot before abruptly turning off the engine. He told Kate that they had a couple of hours to kill before the ferry was due. This frustrated Kate because instead of rushing, she would have preferred to have used that time to savour the precious goodbye of leaving her hometown. Slightly annoyed at Ford, Kate asked him why they had rushed so much.

"Kate," said Ford calmly and slowly. "The ferry service only runs once each day. Use it or lose it."

Kate kept her head down. She was almost grateful for the fact that she had been granted some time before coming face to face with her new home. Equally though, she was so anxious about the whole thing by now that time spent with Ford, where he wasn't really doing much to reassure her, seemed to put her on edge anyway. She couldn't win. Maybe this was the beginnings of a rift between them or maybe she was simply just nervous. She really wished that she had the ability to calm her own mind.

"Come on Kate," Ford seemed to brighten up, thus melting the tension between them. "Let's find somewhere to get some coffee from so we can warm up a bit."

Ford's kindness and control over the situation did something to lift Kate's spirits and take her mind off of her spiralling train of thought.

"I like how you think, Ford," she said, smiling at him as she squeezed his hand.

Once out of the car, Kate looked over the sea. She took in the sounds, the smells and the sights. It was fresh yet cold, calming yet eerie.

"I can't see the island, Ford," she said, baffled.

"You can't see it from here, Kate," Ford clicked his tongue. "Sometimes you really do think too much!"

Kate sensed that there was more that Ford wanted to say to her but that he was holding back for some reason unbeknownst to her. Maybe she was just being paranoid. She had so many hopes, so many dreams. As a new bride, she wanted to live them all. She wanted to be happy. She wanted to share romantic meals with Ford and spend time laughing with him and cuddled up happily together. Perhaps this was all about what it was to be holding the expectations of a new marriage.

"You know that I want you to be happy, don't you Kate?" Ford looked at her pointedly. "Remember that this is all familiar to me, so I do apologise if I seem a bit indifferent. This is new to you and yet, I'm on familiar territory. I promise to welcome you into your new home. Do you understand?"

Kate almost felt guilty about the extent to which she had been questioning Ford, doubting him even. She felt a pang of regret as she reminded herself that she felt a tremendous amount of love for this tall handsome man that stood before her and had made the choice to make her his wife.

They strolled around the port town, with Kate taking in the views whilst Ford kept an eye on his new wife. He felt joyous as he observed the playful lilt with which she walked. It was almost like a skip. It seemed that she was pleased to be out of the car and focused on something more interactive.

He liked the way that her dress sat on her hips and he was attracted to the way that her cardigan came over her wrists and every so often, she would fiddle with the embroidery at the ends of the sleeves. She was an attractive woman in her own way, pale skin and a dimple on one cheek that showed when she smiled. She was very youthful in some ways. She also had an air of loneliness about her. Ford was very aware of the fact that he was really, her only go-to person in the entire world. Not only was he her husband but he was her friend and her mentor.

Kate often wondered what Ford saw in her. She had always been quite the loner and she had never really understood why. It's just how things had seemed to turn out for her. The truth was that Kate was in awe of Ford and there were many times where, over and over in her head, she wondered why he had picked her.

They arrived at the coffee shop. Kate was surprised at how run-down it looked but such was the nature of the area, she supposed. Once they were sat at a round table, covered neatly with a red and white patterned cloth, Ford called over to someone that he was familiar with.

"Hey Simon, come over here and serve us, will you?"

"Welcome back Mr Billson," the man said as he

sauntered over to the table. "What can I get for you? The usual? And how about your girl here, what will she be having?"

"Simon!" Ford swiftly cut in before the man could continue. "I'll have you know that this is my wife! We'll both have a coffee please."

"Oh, give over!" said Simon, somewhat annoyingly. "I heard that you were getting married. News travels fast, you know. I can't believe that you didn't tell us yourself!"

"Kate, this is Simon Green, the self-appointed welcome committee of Springfield," Ford explained to Kate before turning to Simon. "Simon, this is Mrs Billson."

Simon left and soon came back with two coffees. He practically slammed them on the table, making it clutter and wobble. The mugs didn't match, and the coffee looked very weak.

"Hey," he said. "Are you going to be staying on the island? Some of us wondered if you had decided to leave it behind."

"I don't see why I would," replied Ford, his frustration with Simon rising. "I thought I'd made it clear enough that I was just going to be away for a while on business. Anyway, I'm back now so there you have it."

Kate stirred her coffee, slowly but keen to get out of the coffee shop. She was looking forward to the conversion with Simon reaching its natural termination. She found him to be irritating and nosy and she was certain that Ford felt the same. She wasn't wrong.

Simon slapped his palm down on the table, shaking it once more as he leaned in towards Kate and spoke loudly.

"Hey, and you look after yourself once you get to that island, you hear me? Be healthy, be well and be careful." He turned to speak to Ford. "I bet you'll be telling her a few stories about that place. She'll find it interesting, I reckon anyway."

Ford had had enough. He stood up and motioned to Kate by cocking his head towards the coffee shop door that it was time for them to leave.

Chapter Two

With all eyes focused on her, the few steps towards the coffee shop door seemed like such a long time. Kate kept her head held high and continued to look straight in front of her, fixing her gaze on Ford's broad shoulders. They finally passed the door braced on its broken hinges and went down two unsteady steps until they reached the refreshing breeze of the outdoors. Ford's long stride became even broader. Kate found herself almost running in order to keep up with him. As Ford sauntered swiftly towards the docks, Kate had the feeling that not only was he running away from Simon's unwanted comments but also from her.

She called after him to slow down, but Ford continued with determination until he had reached the dock railing. Once there, he leant on it, staring out into the mist where she knew, the island must be.

Finally catching up with him, Kate cautiously slid her hand under his arm. With his body tense and his thoughts concealed, Ford apologised to Kate. He was still uncomfortable, all the more so when Kate finally questioned him.

"What was Simon's problem? He's really upset you."

"The past never leaves," Ford mused. "You can tell yourself that it has but truly, it never does."

Kate looked at Ford quizzically. Ford, seeming uncomfortable about this was quick to change his tone to one that was more jovial and certainly dismissive of Kate's curiosity.

"Oh well," he said. "There's a gossiping wind-up merchant in every town, I suppose."

"It will be dark when we get to the island, won't it?" Kate asked, keen to help change the subject in the interest of keeping her husband happy.

Ford assured Kate that they would get to the island not long after sunset but really, there was nothing that she needed to see urgently anyway. In such regard, he advised her to just relax for the rest of their journey. He felt that she would find out soon enough about the island. Maybe too soon, come to think of it.

Ford told Kate to wait while he went for a brisk walk to gather his thoughts. She didn't fully understand but she respected his choice. As she stared out across the water, she noticed that there was a chill in the air. Her mind started to wander into her fears of being alone. It was a familiar feeling. She had experienced it when her parents had both passed away within a short time of each other. She had been training as a typist at the time. It was a very lonely period in her life. The very people who had stood behind her were no longer championing her and everyone else at college was too busy getting on with their own lives. Kate could go for days without talking to anyone.

It was a profound part of Kate's psyche that she needed to belong. Somewhere. Anywhere. She had moved to the city for a while after college to live with an aunt, but it wasn't long before that changed too. Aunt Melissa, being the eccentric character that she was, had decided to get married again and thus, she put her place up for sale to move in with her new husband. Once again Kate was a spare wheel in a busy world. As a feeble and almost insulting means of compensation, Aunt Melissa gave Kate a ticket to a holiday. A cruise ship of all things. Kate had never been on one before and wasn't sure that she wanted to go but, with little choice and nowhere else to go, Kate found herself amongst the hustle and bustle of annoyingly joyous holiday makers.

The only thing that made the whole event of the cruise ship feel worthwhile was that ultimately, Kate had met Ford there. Ford Billson. He was a good catch. The way the other women on the ship looked at him, it was a widely held opinion that Kate was incredibly lucky to have Ford's attention. Throughout the ten days of the cruise, Ford would always seek Kate out, wanting to talk to her, wanting to spend time with her. Just wanting to be in her presence. She was bowled over. She didn't fully understand but she certainly felt flattered, and maybe even a little comforted. She needed to feel comforted.

Ford was aware – enough to be concerned for her – of Kate's circumstances. He didn't want to let her go. He offered her marriage and he offered her a life with him on the island. He had lived there all of his life. Kate always found it strange how Ford didn't tell her much about the island. His otherwise dynamic demeanour became stoic when she asked him what was perhaps too many questions.

Kate was distracted from her thoughts as she saw Ford walking towards her. Perhaps he had been and had a word with that gossiping moron in the coffee shop. Kate certainly knew better than to ask. Without saying much to each other, Ford and Kate got in the car and they were soon going up the ramp onto the ferry.

Still somewhat bewildered by the events of the last few hours, Kate reminded herself that although she was Ford's wife, she was a separate entity from all of the struggles that had happened in his life before they had met. She made a promise to herself that she would stay strong for her husband.

A good while later, something came up suddenly on the horizon as the ferry moved further towards it. It was the island. It was smallish but enchanting all the same. Kate's new home. It was certainly different to anything that she had ever seen before but maybe that didn't matter. She was here with her husband after all. Still though, it wasn't the most conventional-looking place to call home.

After driving for not too long at all, the journey took them along a narrow dirt road. Out of the window, although it was dusk, Kate could see a little bit of the waterfront. Rocks made shapes in the shadows. It looked almost ghostly.

Chapter Three

The house was… beautiful. But in a twisted way. Kate couldn't find a word that best described how she felt about it. It was a huge house, sitting on a large expanse of land. Once upon a time, it had white marble pillars, but they had whitewashed with age. Still, it retained its glory with its huge windows and doors and a balcony which overlooked the entrance. Someone had let the garden grow out of control and the vines intertwined over pillars and windows, rising up as if in a delicate pattern which created a sort of poignancy.

Kate turned around, just as the black wrought iron gates closed. She walked to the fountain that sat in the middle of the compound. Just like the house, it was old and covered in vines. It seemed to be a mockery of what it used to be, completely dry with pebbles. She looked up and gulped. Staring at her were two ornamental creatures. They looked like gargoyles, but with maniacal faces that sent a chill through her body.

"Welcome home," Ford said.

She looked up at her husband. Husband! She couldn't believe she was married. It just seemed so incredible. Just months ago she had been so alone. If anyone had told her she would be married, she would have told them they were crazy. However, the huge diamond on her finger was proof of her new status.

"It is…"

"Old?" Ford said with a grin. The same grin that had attracted her the day they met.

She nodded. Although he had not told her much about his home, she hadn't expected it to be this way. Old and spooky. No effort had been made, but it was a perfect prop for a horror movie. She wouldn't be surprised if the door was opened by a floating butler.

"This home has been in my family for generations," Ford said.

That he had told her. She had expected an old and sturdy house, but she hadn't expected it to be in such disrepair. He was a wealthy man, with power at his fingertips. It would take him nothing to renovate the house.

The front door opened, and two men hurried out. She was disappointed that they were ordinary men. Tall thin men, one with long dark hair left to roam wild, and the other with a buzz cut. They were dressed in black trousers and braces.

"Master Ford, welcome," the taller of them said with a nod.

"Isaac, you got my message I believe?" Ford asked.

"Yes sir. The house is prepared," he said.

Ford made the introductions and the men drew their attention towards Kate. She wondered what they saw. Did they approve of her? Ford was a good-looking man. At six foot and two inches, he hovered over her much shorter height. He was well-built, although he lacked the swelling muscles of weightlifters. His hair was dark and curly, long enough for her fingers to go through with content. And his face? It was a work of art. A well-chiselled face, an aristocratic nose as she liked to call it, and the darkest eyes she had ever seen. He radiated a powerful aura, and no matter where he went, both men and women would stare at him.

Kate was pretty, but not to the extent that she was exceptional. She was slender with long legs and was quite busty for her stature. Her dark hair was a mess some days. She had been told she had the girl-next-door beauty, whatever that meant. She wasn't like those exotic models or women who others gazed upon. In a pool of women, she was easily forgettable. But she didn't mind. She had long ago realised that there was more to a person than their looks.

There was a huge lobby with a chandelier overhead. It led into a huge living room with the doors and windows opening into a courtyard. Just like the house, the furniture was old. It would be paradise for anyone with an interest in antiques.

"How old is this house again?" Kate asked.

"Over four hundred years," said Silas, the butler, looking bookish with thin glasses perched on his nose.

Ford had told Kate that most of the staff had worked for his parents and he had inherited them. It all felt like royalty and she wouldn't be surprised if she had a chambermaid waiting for her.

Four hundred years was pretty old. Kate doubted she had any heirloom that went that far back.

"Isaac will take you to your room, while I settle down in mine," Ford said.

"Different rooms? But… we are married," Kate said, dismayed.

It seemed the staff disappeared into thin air, or they had mastered the act of being invisible when their master attended to personal affairs.

"Yes, we are married," Ford said as he caressed her face. "But you need a space of your own. I want you to enjoy all that this house has to offer. The beauty. The service. Besides, you are tired. You have had a long day. You need all the rest you can get."

He was right in that regard. She was indeed very tired. Travelling here had taken hours. First had been the wedding, then being waltzed away to the island. She stifled a yawn. She wanted to argue about them having separate rooms, but she was too tired for that. Besides, not in front of the staff.

"I will stop by your room soon," Ford said, kissing her head.

Her eyes widened as Isaac led her to what he called the west wing, where her room was. She could hear their footsteps as they went down the hallway. It was just so quiet – so much so that it had her looking over her shoulder. Perhaps sensing her fears, Isaac spoke.

"The last time the house was fully occupied was

over thirty years ago, when Master Ford's parents were alive. Since then, the house has been quiet. Most of the rooms are covered up and filled with dust and cobwebs."

"How do I not get lost?" she muttered.

Isaac laughed.

"You will find your way mistress," he said. "It is easy to navigate through the house, and you will have servants at your beck and call."

Mistress? Servants? It felt like she had been tossed into the nineteenth century. But then Ford came from an old family and with what he had told her, they stuck to tradition. She just hadn't expected it to be this grand.

They stopped at the end of the hallway, in front of double oak doors. Isaac pushed the doors open and she walked into what was her room. She loved it immediately. There was a huge Victorian bed with posters. Arranging the bed was a young woman with her hair in a bun, dressed in a pink uniform.

She curtseyed and Kate smiled. She guessed she had to get used to this sort of treatment.

"This is Beth. She will be one of your close aides," Isaac introduced.

"Mistress," Beth nodded.

Kate's bags had already been brought in and were sat by the bed. She walked past them and toured her room. The bathroom was three times the size of her former bathroom. She lifted a brow at what she saw. Was that gold on the handle and seat? There was a huge claw-footed bathtub and a mirror. The wallpapers were faded but they had once been pink. She emerged and checked out her closet. It was not what she expected. It was filled with clothes, shoes, bags and accessories. The clothes and shoes were her size. Beautiful clothes. She marvelled as she ran her fingers through a few. Should she be surprised? Ford was that way. Thoughtful. Controlling.

She thought back to when they had first met. How out of all the beautiful women on the cruise ship, he had picked her. How he had held her confidently as they danced on the deck. How his overbearing mystique was intoxicating, even if a little overwhelming. Ford was a man who wouldn't waste his own time. Ford was a man who would only go for something if he truly wanted it. And of all those things, he wanted her. He wanted Kate.

Although their courtship had been short, whenever he was around, he was a present figure in her life. And then he had proposed. Some said she was crazy to accept his proposal, and even crazier to want to get married to him so soon. But there was no need to wait. Why wait? She had wanted this for so long. A love so beautiful that it made her both scared and happy at the same time. As they were pronounced man and wife, she had known getting married to Ford was the right thing. They were meant to be.

Chapter Four

It was dark when Kate woke up. She tossed around in the comfortable bed. Her stomach rumbled and she realised she hadn't had anything to eat apart from a sandwich on the ferry. She had been too tired to go down for supper. She checked the time on the clock that was sitting on the side table. She had slept for over four hours. She must have been more tired than she had realised.

The window was closed, but the room still felt chilly. She got off the bed and went out onto the balcony. She gasped as the cold air hit her. As Ford had said, it could be very windy here. The island was small and just off the coast. It was home to a close-knit community, some of whom were old families. The others were families that had served them for years. They were mostly farmers, and exportation was a huge source of income.

Kate smiled as she thought back to the conversations she'd had with herself when it had properly dawned on her that she would be living on the island. *It's pretty much in the middle of nowhere! Are you crazy?* she'd asked herself.

No, she wasn't crazy. But she knew it sounded crazy to leave the familiar and come all the way here. But she had nothing to lose. Her parents had died years ago, and she was an only child. She was used to her own company. And her extended family? Well, maybe they were out there somewhere and she would feel some kind of love for them because they were family; uncles, aunts, and cousins, maybe anyway. Either way though, Kate had never felt like she truly belonged. She had always yearned for her space, a family of her own. And she was going to have that with Ford.

The island was pretty quiet. As she stood on the balcony, Kate could see a couple of lights spread out in the night. But it was oddly quiet. She had once visited a holiday island when she was a little girl, and in the night, voices and laughter from other visitors drifted around. But here, it felt like she was all alone.

Ford was a well-respected man. His authority was based on his capabilities, even though he did have a domineering presence about him. He was a quietly assured man who had nothing to prove.

Kate had always known there was nothing mean about him. He could be cold, but he loved her, and that was all that mattered.

Her stomach rumbled again, and she realised that she was hungry to the point of distraction and it could no longer be ignored.

As she reached for the handle, it twisted, as if someone had tried to reach for it at the same time. However, when the door opened, there was no one on the other side. The door was probably stiff, she assumed, as she headed back the way she had come earlier on.

The hallways were lit with dim lights, but they were bright enough for her to find her way. The bumps on her arms rose and she felt her heart race. She suddenly stopped and looked over her shoulder. She didn't know what it was, but it felt like there was someone behind her. She turned around but couldn't see anyone. Faster, she continued down the hallway with a strange feeling that a presence was following her.

She was relieved when she burst out into the landing, almost running into a maid. She apologised and hurried down the stairs. Ford sat at the head of the table flipping through an old book with faded pages.

"How was your rest? I figured you would be hungry, but you needed your rest more," Ford said.

"I rested well," Kate said.

She wanted to tell him about the experience on the way, but she dismissed it. It was probably her imagination running wild.

"Are you ok?"

"Yes, but very hungry."

At this, Ford rang a bell, and in a matter of seconds, a feast was spread before them. She marvelled at the spread; she could feast on this for a week and this was just for the two of them as one meal!

"This is way too much! It will all go to waste," she said with a frown.

She might not have grown up in the drenches of poverty, but she hated waste.

"The staff will share what's left," Ford said simply.

Ford's nonchalant attitude did little to reassure Kate.

"They should eat whenever they deem fit, and we don't have to fill the table up when it is just the two of us eating," Kate said.

"I will talk to Silas. He will not like the change, but you are the mistress of the house now," Ford said.

As they ate, she tried to raise conversation. She asked about the island and the house. It disappointed her that Ford's answers were curt, his mind far away. He was not a talker, but she expected him to interact more than he did. It was more like she was talking to herself.

They moved into the living room after dinner, her hand in his.

"Do you have friends on the island?" she asked.

"Yes, I do. A few. Men and women I grew up with. They will find you amazing," he said, smiling.

"Won't they find it odd that none of them were invited to the wedding?"

It had worried her that none of his family or friends had come for the wedding. She had insisted but he had claimed it would be too much of an inconvenience to bring them over. A quiet registry office signing with just two business associates as witnesses had been enough for him.

"We could throw a party, so I can get introduced to everyone," Kate suggested.

He pulled away from her.

"A party? This house hasn't seen a party in a long time. It is a nice suggestion. Discuss it with Silas," he said, looking at his wristwatch. "I will stop by your room. I have some business to attend to."

She watched him as he walked off, leaving her alone in the middle of the almost dark living room. He had more or less just dismissed her. She shook her head disbelievingly. Fine, he hadn't actually showered her with much attention before, but he had never treated her like she didn't matter. He was probably tired she told herself. Tomorrow, things would be different.

Chapter Five

Despite having gone to bed early, Kate felt like she had barely slept a wink. The night had been strange. She had woken up at several intervals, sensing that she wasn't alone. It had felt as if someone was at the foot of her bed, staring at her, but when she put the bedside lamp on, there was no one there. After that, she had left the light on. Yet, she had still felt uncomfortable. She had checked the closet and the bathroom, even under the bed, but no one else was there. Every time she'd managed to fall asleep, she woke up to that eerie feeling. A few times she heard footsteps that had stopped right in front of her door. She had also heard strange noises from outside; probably a wild animal but the sounds made her lock the windows. Then there were the strange dreams; she couldn't recall them in the morning, but they had brought her out of sleep several times.

There was a knock on the door and Beth walked

in, holding a tray of breakfast.

"Good morning mistress, I trust you had a good night," she smiled.

Kate nodded. A good night indeed! She had never felt so uncomfortable in her life.

"How long have you worked here?" she asked Beth.

"Seven years. My aunt worked here, and when she died, I was hired," Beth said with pride.

And you sleep well at night? Kate wanted to ask, but she restrained herself. Unlike Ford, Beth was forthcoming with information. Most of the families on the island were rich; they came from old money which never seemed to run dry. The island was divided between the rich, and those who served the rich. They rarely left the island, and when they did, they always returned home, even if they had businesses far away. With the finances of the families, they had adequate facilities, including a market and a church.

"And tourists?"

Beth frowned at this.

"We don't like strangers," she said, speaking quickly upon seeing Kate's surprise. "Tourists, they come here, they take pictures and leave. Not many come here. We are very quiet. No fun, so they don't come here."

That calmed Kate a little, although she could still feel there was more to it than that. She had more questions to ask but her husband walked in. Beth took the tray and hurried away. Kate smiled in amusement; the staff either feared or respected him.

"What's so funny?" Ford asked, sitting next to her.

"I don't know whether to be amused that they seem to fear you," she said.

"They should," he said.

Her brow lifted at this.

"Don't expect me to," she said.

Ford laughed, his smile grew wider and his eyes lit up. The beautiful sound made Kate's heart swell with happiness. She loved watching him laugh.

"There's no need to fear me. I hope you slept well," he said, taking her hand in his.

"No, I didn't," she said, shaking her head. "I had nightmares. And there were sounds; it was like there was someone in here with me."

All amusement disappeared from Ford's face.

"Someone was in here with you?" he asked coldly.

"I think so. I put the light on and there was no one. I checked everywhere. It was probably my imagination. You know I was tired," she said quickly, not wanting to upset him.

"You should familiarise yourself with the estate," Ford said. He looked at his watch and he sighed. "I have a few stops to make, but I will be with you by lunch."

She wanted him to be with her all day, but he was a businessman with many strings to his bow. She kissed him, not wanting to let go. When he walked away, it felt like a part of her went with him.

She stayed in bed much longer, trying to catch up on her lost sleep, but it was no use. She had told Ford the restlessness was from tiredness, but she didn't think so. It had been much more than that and she couldn't explain it, not even to herself.

Not wanting to stay in bed all morning, she went on a tour of the estate. It was even bigger than she had thought. Isaac was by her side as he showed her around. The estate was indeed old, but renovations were done from time to time. A river ran through and he pointed towards a direction, where there were ruins from hundreds of years ago.

Most of the estate remained unused, he said. He also introduced her to the staff, starting with the household. There was a huge barn with beautiful horses with long manes; she didn't know how to ride, and Isaac said he was sure his master would want her to learn. He led her to the farms, it was harvest season and she watched as wheat was cut by the labourers. It was a new experience for her. She had always been a city girl at heart, and now she had been thrust into a rural life, albeit one of luxury. It would take some time for her to get used to it, but she was sure she would figure it out.

"As the mistress of the house, the house is under your care, whatever changes you want to make, I am at your service," Isaac said with a bow.

As they rounded back to the house, Kate decided that it seemed ok the way it was. Despite it being her home, she wasn't here to intrude. She would see how things were and if they needed a change, then there would be.

She lazed around for a while, but there was nothing fun to do in the big house. So, she found herself in the library which was in the quiet east wing. The library was filled with old books, some of which were in a strange language. She found a William Shakespeare book and pulled it out, settling into an armchair. It was one of her favourites, *The Merchant of Venice*, and she was looking forward to a great read that would bring back the images that had danced in her head when she'd first read it.

She was on the second act when she noticed something. The room was getting colder; it was like someone had opened every single window in the building, even though this wasn't the case. Precipitation was beginning to appear on the windows. And then, the door flung open. She gasped, holding tightly onto the book.

"Who's there?" she called.

She got no answer. Slowly, with her heart pounding so fast she could hear it, she approached the door. She stepped into the hallway. There was nobody there. It must have been the wind, she consoled herself, even though she knew there was no way the wind could have opened the door, not like that.

Her eyes widened when she returned to the library. The chair she had once occupied had been moved. Before, it had been on the right-hand side of the table, and now it was on the left. In the short minute she had gone to the door, the chair had been moved. How was that even possible? Goosebumps rose on her arms as the room got even colder. And then she felt it, a presence. Without a second thought, she ran. She ran out of the room and smack into a column. Her mouth opened in a cry.

"Kate? What's wrong with you? You are shaking," Ford said, his hands on her shoulder.

"There was someone in the library," she blurted out fearfully.

"The library is off-limits. The servants know better than to be in there," Ford said, frowning.

He took her hand and hesitantly she followed him back into the library. Her eyes narrowed. The chair was back to its original position, the cold was gone, and so was the precipitation. It was as if she had imagined the whole thing. Ford looked around but there was nobody.

"There's no one here. Perhaps it was a rat you heard. As much as we try to get rid of them, they can create a ruckus," Ford said with a kind smile.

Her eyes darted past him and stopped on the table. The book was no longer there. With a racing heart, she walked towards the shelf she had pulled it out from. The book was in its place. This was no imagination of hers. Something crazy was going on here.

"Kate," Ford said.

She hugged him tight, relieved that he had arrived at that moment. Something could have happened to her. She shuddered at the feeling.

"I am here love," Ford said, running his fingers through her hair.

It was the most affection he'd shown his wife since they'd arrived on the island.

Chapter Six

The next morning, Ford had left her room in the early hours. Kate wasn't comfortable with this arrangement. They were husband and wife and he didn't need to sneak off like he was committing a crime. Still though, she smiled as she rolled over onto the other side of the bed. There had been no nightmares, or strange events. In his arms she'd slept well. She covered her mouth as a yawn escaped it. Then she reached for the duvet to cover her body, as the morning sun filtered in.

Beth soon arrived and Kate felt ready to start her day. First breakfast, then she had all the time to laze about. She wondered how long this would last. She wasn't used to this lifestyle, doing nothing. No matter how silly it seemed, she needed to keep busy.

For the rest of the day, she made sure she was with

someone else at all times, refusing to be shooed out of the kitchen by the cook. Being alone meant something strange would happen, she could just feel it.

The day ticked along quickly and night crept in. Dinner had been reduced to a smaller portion, one that she was more comfortable with, even though she would have preferred having dinner on a small table, rather than the long table which seemed fit for royalty.

"I will stop by your room," Ford said, getting up from the table.

Her glare followed him. He confused her. One moment he was warm, the next he was cold. Back on the cruise ship he had shown her so much love, and now she just couldn't read him.

She didn't want to be in her room alone. She hoped he would drop by soon. She opened the window for some fresh air and then climbed into the bed. Quickly, her eyes drifted to a close. She had no idea how long she slept for, but she heard a sound, like a flutter. Her eyes sprang open to see that there, on the end of her bed, sat a large black crow.

Kate screamed in surprise, but the noise did not stir the crow from its perch. The stark bird stared at her with deep, glassy eyes which mirrored the reflection of her terrified face.

Just as she was about to scream again, her door burst wide open. Ford ran in, followed by Isaac and a few others.

"What happened?" Ford asked, his arms around her.

She pointed at the window. She had woken up to see a crow on her bed. And the bird had stared right at her, watching her. Even when she screamed it hadn't flown off. Only right before the door had been barged open had it flown off, out of the window and into the night.

"I can't sleep alone," Kate shivered.

Ford waved everyone away and settled next to her.

"There is an explanation for this, I am sure," he said to her as he stroked her hair gently in an attempt to calm her.

Kate was anything but calm. Truthfully, she hadn't understood any of the happenings on the island since she'd got there – nor her husband's cold and distant behaviour.

Chapter Seven

Ford was back to being distant in the morning. He didn't seem to want to talk at all, even though Kate was set on discussing what had happened the night before. So, since he was preoccupied with work again, she decided that she would take Isaac up on his offer to escort her on a walk through the gardens. Kate had spent a little time in the gardens since first arriving here, but Isaac had said there was even more to see that she had missed. The sections of the gardens that she had encountered so far were all run-down and overgrown, but he'd promised that there was a place on the grounds that was lush with wildflowers and beautiful scenery. Kate excitedly hoped it was true; she felt ready for some peaceful beauty after last night's encounter with that dreadful crow. To think that a crow would fly all the way inside her bedroom in order to land at the foot of her bed. Kate had told Isaac that she didn't think she had even left the window open, which made the incident all the more alarming. But he said that she had, and just didn't remember. He told her that he had closed the window after everyone had rushed in to see if she was ok. It was all so disturbing that Kate wasn't even sure if she was remembering events correctly anymore.

"Good morning mistress," Isaac said.

Meeting Kate in the foyer, he handed her a cup of tea to bring along on their walk.

"Good morning, Isaac," Kate said. "I would feel much more comfortable if you would just call me Kate, especially now that we have got to know each other a bit more."

"I'm not sure that the master of the house would approve of that," he dutifully replied.

"Well, Ford says that I can make the rules here now too. So, I would like you to call me Kate, if that's ok with you."

"Of course, Kate," Isaac said as he bowed his head towards her slightly.

"Perfect, I'm ready to see the beautiful gardens you have told me about," she smiled.

"Right this way," Isaac said.

He motioned his hand towards the doorway, and

they walked out into the cool, fresh air.

The hot cup of tea was a nice touch. It made Kate feel warm on the inside of her chest as she swallowed long sips of it, which was a nice contrast to the crisp air biting at her cheeks and hands. They walked through the gardens that she remembered having seen before, the ones that looked in disarray, and then a bit further over to some cobblestone paths that looked like they had been laid by hand a very long time ago. There were patches of soft, thick moss growing up between the stones, adding pops of emerald green between the damp grey. When they got to the end of one of the walkways, Isaac stepped to the side in order to let Kate turn the corner first. She stepped around the corner and was delighted by the sight that met her. This garden was every bit as charming as she had hoped it would be.

"Oh Isaac," Kate said. "This is gorgeous!"

He smiled when he saw how pleased she was.

"But how is it that this little hidden garden is so beautiful, and the main garden is such a mess?" she asked him.

"This garden is tended strictly by me in my off-hours when I am not servicing the other needs of the house. I've always liked gardening."

He walked over and sat down on a stone bench that had wrought iron wings affixed to it as armrests. Kate sat down beside him and took in the sights and smells of the wildflowers in the garden. She was completely at ease until she heard a jarring cawing coming from behind her. She turned around quickly to find herself face-to-face with a large crow. It had to be the one from last night, it had to be! She could feel it. She jumped up from the bench and started to shriek as she pointed to the bird, who again did not seem at all affected by her reaction to it.

"Isaac look! Can you see it? The crow is back again."

Isaac turned his head slowly around to look at the crow without getting up from the bench.

"So he is," he replied. "Perhaps he is enjoying the garden this morning as well."

"But, doesn't it make you nervous?" she asked.

"No, not at all."

Isaac looked at the crow almost as if it was an old friend. Then he gave his hand a small wave towards the bird and it lifted up its wings and flew away. Kate wished it had flown away when she had screamed at it.

"Come," Isaac said. "Sit back down."

When Kate returned to the bench, she still had an uneasy feeling over her shoulder; the kind a person might get when they've just had a spider crawling on them and even though they know it has gone, there's a residual twitching on their skin that just won't seem to leave.

"You know," Isaac said as if he was about to tell her a story. "Crows are a very special animal."

"I thought they were the harbingers of bad luck," Kate said.

"Oh no," Isaac laughed. "That's just an old myth, there's no truth to that. Actually, crows are a very intelligent and very spiritual animal."

"*Spiritual?*"

"Yes. They are said to be the connection between life and death. They can fly between the land of the living and the land of the dead in order to communicate with both sides."

"Why would any animal want to visit death?" Kate asked.

"They are messengers," Isaac continued. "They deliver messages to those still alive from loved ones beyond the grave."

"But they can't speak."

"They speak with their presence. They speak with signs from the beyond."

It started to freak Kate out a bit that Isaac seemed to be so comfortable with the bird that had nearly scared her to death in her bedroom.

"What sign is this bird giving to me?" she asked, knowing that she probably didn't want to know the answer even as she asked it.

"That death is near," Isaac replied.

"Oh my God! What?!" Kate gasped.

Isaac chuckled but she wasn't sure what was so funny.

"I'm just teasing," he said. "The bird is probably just looking for some insects to eat. Come, let's go back inside the house now."

Kate was not at all amused. She was pleased that Isaac seemed more comfortable and less formal around her now, but she was completely offended that he took her distress so lightly. Isaac may have been an old and faithful servant of Ford's family, but he sometimes gave her the creeps. Just like many things in the old house did.

They didn't talk much on the walk back. He

pointed to various plants and things along the way and asked her a few benign questions about what she would like for dinner over the course of the next few meals. Kate was listening to him, mostly, but she was also keeping a keen and cautious lookout for the crow. She didn't like the feeling that something was always watching her here. She missed being in a town with a lot of people. At least there, someone would always hear a call for help, and there weren't crows flying into the houses.

When they reached the house again, Isaac excused himself to go back to work on his duties and left Kate alone with her thoughts. She went to go and find Ford, who it emerged was at his desk in the study looking over various export ledgers and sighing to himself.

"What are you doing?" Kate asked.

She smiled and walked up to him, putting her hand on the back of his shoulder as he worked.

"Working," was his single-worded response.

"Isaac took me for a walk through the gardens this morning," she continued. "He showed me the small, special garden towards the back of the house. It's really beautiful and the wildflowers were really…"

"Kate," Ford said abruptly. "I'm working."

He lifted his chin up just high enough to show that he was addressing her but didn't turn his head to look in her direction. His demeanour was again, cold and distant, and even harsh.

"I'm sorry," she said.

She removed her hand from his shoulder and left the study. Thoughts of second-guessing her decision to come here started to creep up in her mind, and as much as she tried to push them back down, this time they lingered.

Kate spent the rest of the day sitting on the balcony of her bedroom, looking out at the water and the clouds in the sky. She thought about the life she had left behind, and about how frayed her nerves had been since she got here. She also thought about how much she loved Ford. It soon helped her to talk herself down from at least some of her paranoia. Ford was her husband, and a good man. He had given her no reason to fear that he would be cruel or unfaithful to her. And like he had told her; it would take her some time to get adjusted to a new home and a new life. That was all it was, and she just needed to give it some more time.

When Beth popped her head into Kate's bedroom to see if she needed anything, Kate was ready to ask for a glass of wine. Beth smiled before she left and then returned within minutes with a tall glass of white wine which she held atop a silver tray.

See, Kate thought to herself. *This is really all wonderful. I just need to relax.*

Dinner seemed to be one of the few times that Kate knew without a doubt she would see her husband. No matter what his workload seemed to be, he would always make sure to meet Kate at the dinner table so that the two of them could talk and spend time together. She still hated how long the table was and how far apart they had to sit. She didn't want to bring it up to him again now, but she reminded herself that at some point during the next few days, she wanted to make a new seating arrangement; one in which she didn't feel like a client in a boardroom.

"How was your afternoon?" Ford asked her from across the table.

"It was fine," Kate replied.

"Just *fine*?" he asked as he put a piece of steak in his mouth.

"I was hoping that I would have been able to spend more time with you."

The tone of Kate's voice sounded sad enough to make Ford notice. A slight look of remorse crossed his face.

"Yes, I'm sorry about that," he said as he continued to chew the meat which had been seasoned to perfection. "My workload this week is exceedingly burdensome. In fact, I need to be gone for a day on business."

"Gone where?" Kate asked, setting her glass down as she looked at him with concern.

"It's nothing far away, just about town a bit. It won't take me long. I shouldn't be away for more than a day."

"I don't want to stay here alone," Kate said adamantly.

"Don't be ridiculous," he said as he washed down his food with a big gulp of wine. "This is your home now."

"That may be so, but I still don't feel comfortable here."

Ford looked discouraged, which was at least a sign that he cared.

"Tell me what I can do to make you more comfortable here in *our* home," he said.

"You can take me with you on your business trip, or not go at all," Kate replied. "I don't want to be left behind."

"I can't take you with me on a business trip, and I do have to go. But how about this; I promise that I will make the trip as fast as I possibly can. And I will also see to it that all of the servants increase their presence in the house with you while I am gone. Ok?"

It wasn't what Kate wanted. She wanted him to stay with her. But it was better than nothing, so she accepted. He wasn't scheduled to leave for a few more days anyway, so at least they would be able to spend some time together first.

"So," Ford continued as he changed the subject. "Tell me all about the garden that you saw today."

The change of topic worked, and they spent the better part of the evening talking and laughing and sipping wine together. Even though it was still unsettling how Ford managed to go from being aloof and callous to being attentive and caring, it was easy for Kate to forget about the negative things when she and Ford were spending happy and tender moments together. When he was right there beside her, it was easy for her to forget about what being alone in this house felt like.

Chapter Eight

When Ford left for business a few days later, Kate was left alone in the house. Well, not completely alone, but she felt alone enough. She had slept in late that morning; knowing that Ford was away, she had no real reason to get up. She didn't want to spend the day by herself in the house. When she heard Beth come in to check on her for what must have been the dozenth time, she opened her eyes.

"Good morning, mistress," Beth said, relieved that Kate was now finally awake.

"Please, Beth, call me Kate," she yawned.

She sat up in bed and squinted at the sun coming through the foggy morning outside.

Beth looked uncomfortable, but she always looked a little anxious anyway.

"Is everything ok, Beth?"

"Yes, mistre… I mean, Kate. Everything is fine. Can I bring you some coffee?"

"Yes please," Kate said, not entirely convinced.

Beth returned a few minutes later with a steaming cup of coffee, but when she stepped into the bedroom, she froze. Her attention was directly focused on the window as if she could see something there. Kate watched as all the colour seemed to drain from Beth's cheeks.

"Beth?" she asked as she pushed her blankets aside and stood up from the bed to walk over to her. "Is something wrong?"

Beth didn't answer. She just stood staring at the window, as if she had seen a ghost. When Kate was standing directly in front of her and taking the cup from her hands, Beth finally snapped out of it.

"Sorry," she said. "The sunrise was just so pretty to look at that I got lost for a moment."

Kate turned and looked out the window.

"But the sunrise was well over a while ago," she said as she looked back at Beth with doubt and confusion. "And besides, it's cloudy and overcast now."

Beth appeared not to know what to say, so instead she just nodded her head and then scurried off.

Strange.

After she had got dressed, Kate decided to occupy her time by doing some re-decorating. She was still bothered by the table in the dining room, so she thought she would set up a smaller, more intimate dining area for herself and Ford to enjoy.

There was so much furniture scattered around the house that it was easy to come up with a smaller table and some chairs. She dragged the small table in from another one of the rooms and then followed with two chairs that had extremely comfortable-looking cushions on them. There was a nook in the corner of the vast dining room that she thought would be perfect for the new arrangement.

Kate stood back and looked at the table and chairs, pleased with herself, and then went off to the linen closets and service hutch to find a tablecloth and some place settings. She was sure that Ford would be pleased with her efforts, even if at first, he got mad about the change. She smiled as she thought about being able to sit closer to him and engage in deeper conversations.

When she got to the linen closets and opened them, she found large stacks of white tablecloths and napkins and even some beautiful lace accents that she could put on the centre of the table to arrange a vase of flowers on. She grabbed onto a tablecloth and pulled it out, trying not to topple down the rest of the linens as she did so. It wasn't until she had the tablecloth halfway pulled out that she noticed the crimson red stains streaking the white fabric. For a moment, she was in too much shock for it to register, and she foolishly wondered how spilled wine could have made such a deep red mess. Then she realised it wasn't wine at all.

She screamed and dropped the blood-soaked linen to the floor. All of the other fabrics came falling out from the closet with it. She looked at her hands to see if they had any blood on them as well, but they looked completely clean.

Beth came running through the hall and stopped short when she saw Kate in front of the open closet.

"What is it?" Beth asked breathlessly. "What's wrong?"

"There's blood drenching that tablecloth," Kate said as she lifted a shaking finger to point towards the white linen.

Beth timidly lifted the other pieces on top of it until she had reached the tablecloth that Kate was pointing to. She uncovered it and even opened it up in her arms. The cloth was clean; pure white and spotless.

"This one?" Beth asked, looking confused. "Are you sure?"

Kate stared at the sheet of white that was outstretched in Beth's arms. There was no blood on it – not a single drop.

"I swear I saw it," Kate muttered, sounding almost hysterical. "There was red blood all over that tablecloth."

Beth folded the tablecloth back up and carefully put all the linens back into the closet.

"Are you feeling unwell?" she asked as she closed the closet doors and turned to Kate. "Perhaps you should lie down."

"No!" Kate shouted at her. "I am fine. It's this house that is unwell."

She stomped off back towards the dining room, leaving Beth to stand in the hall with a perplexed expression.

When Kate got back to the dining room, she had to cover her mouth to keep from screaming again. The table and chairs that she had placed so perfectly in the corner of the room, were now set upon the long dining room table with their legs poking straight up in the air. Kate was just as frightened as she was angry. Perhaps someone was playing a trick on her; maybe one of the servants was disgruntled by something her husband had done and tormenting her was their way to get revenge on him. Or, perhaps not. Either way, it didn't seem like anyone believed that there was actually something going on in the house. Kate didn't even have anyone who she could call to talk about it with. Every time she screamed or even tried to tell someone about the things she saw, they all just looked at her with pity as though she was some kind of lunatic who needed consoling.

Kate reached up and pulled the table and chairs down from the dining table and set them back in the alcove where she had put them before. She was not going to be some scared little girl in her own home, not if she could help it anyway. She decided to forgo the tablecloth and instead she pulled place settings out of the hutch and arranged them nicely on the table top, leaving space for some flowers that she would go and collect from the garden later.

She needed to find a book to read, something that she could put her thoughts into and take her mind off the rest of the day trapped alone in the house with her paranoia. She knew Ford had said the library was off-limits, and she knew he'd be mad if he caught her going in there again. But she felt it was ridiculous to prevent her from getting a single book to read. Kate wasn't keen herself on going back into that room, not after what had happened the last time.

Just as she had started to make her way down the hallway, Kate saw Isaac coming from the corridor that led to the library. She thought that was odd, considering that Ford had told her no one was allowed in that room, not even the staff. She quickly changed course and acted as if she was walking towards her bedroom instead. She didn't want to have to explain to Isaac where she was going, and she also didn't want to hear any more of his creepy stories. She went into her room for a few minutes to wait until the path was clear again.

The sound of faint conversation came from just outside her door. Carefully, Kate went to press her ear against it to listen to what was being said. It was difficult to make out the words, but she could tell that it was Isaac and the other male butler that she had seen when she'd first arrived at the house.

"Does she know?" the other man asked.

"No," Isaac answered curtly. "And it's best for everyone's sake that she doesn't find out."

Kate tried to silence the sound of her breathing for

fear that they might hear her on the other side of the door. After a few silent moments, she heard the sound of footsteps walking away from her room in two separate directions. She waited for a few more minutes and then opened the door carefully so as not to make any squeaks or creaks. She cautiously poked her head out from the doorway and looked down both sides of the hall. When she saw that no one was there, she started walking back to the library again. She was troubled by what she had heard and wondered what the two men had meant. What was it that they didn't want her to find out about? She should have just opened the door right then and there and confronted them. She should have demanded to know what they were discussing. But it was hard to be brave when she felt so unsettled.

When Kate reached the library, she took one more look back at the hallway behind her to make sure that no one had seen her sneak inside. She would make this as quick and as quiet as she could do and would then return to her room with a book, or maybe even her balcony again so that she could read in the cool air under the cloudy sky. The door was soundless as she opened it, no creaks or moans from the hinges, which she was grateful for. But just as she slid inside and went to look up at the shelves lined with stories for her to choose from, she stifled a cry when she saw Ford, sitting there at the small table in the library, with his nose in a book. He looked up at her with a blank expression on his face when he saw her come into the room.

"What are you doing in here?" she asked him.

It took Ford a moment to answer her, almost as if his mind had been asleep and needed to restart.

"I could ask you the same thing," he said.

"No," Kate shouted, determined this time not to leave without getting some answers. "You cannot blame me for coming into the forbidden library, when you yourself are sitting in here after you told me you would be away from the house all day. I thought you had business to attend to in town?"

"I did," Ford said casually. "But then I finished it and came home."

"But…" Kate was almost too upset to put her words together. "How could you be finished already? It's only been a couple of hours. And why wouldn't you tell me that you were home instead of coming in here to read?"

"I was tired," Ford said as he set his book down on the table next to him. "I just needed a moment of quiet."

"And you have that little regard for me, that you

would ignore my worries in this house and think only of yourself?" Kate was nearly on the verge of tears.

"Of course not," Ford said as he stood up from his seat.

His behaviour was so odd. It was as if he was cold and uncaring, while at the same time trying to be loving and protective. There was no explanation that he could give that would effectively explain to Kate the way he had been acting.

"It is because I have such high regard for you that I stayed away."

"What?" Kate's eyes widened as if she found herself talking to a madman.

"What's all the commotion in here, sir?" Isaac called from behind Kate.

She flung around to see him standing in the doorway.

"Nothing, Isaac," Ford answered him. "I was just getting ready to head towards the study to get some more work done."

Isaac nodded as Ford walked past Kate, giving her a small kiss on the cheek before walking out of the room.

"Everything ok, Kate?" Isaac asked, casually turning the thick gold band on his finger around with his thumb.

This time when he called her by her first name, it sent chills up her spine.

Chapter Nine

Beth joined Kate for breakfast the next morning. Kate hadn't gone down for dinner the night before, and when Ford had visited her room to check on her, she had given him the cold shoulder as best she could. She hated acting that way towards her husband, but honestly, things had to change. She shouldn't be made to feel uneasy in her own home, or unwanted in her own marriage.

Beth seemed better than she had been the previous day; not as skittish, not as on edge. Kate wasn't really sure if she was keen on having breakfast with her, but she felt it was the least she could do seeing that Beth had offered an olive branch.

"So, where do you and the other staff stay?" Kate asked out of pure curiosity. "Are your quarters here in the main house?"

"Yes, we stay on the ground floor in the wing that leads off from the kitchen," Beth said, nodding her head as she sipped her tea.

"I didn't know there was such a wing."

"It's not something that your husband likes to put on the tour," Beth giggled.

She was kind of funny, and as close to a friend as Kate had in the house.

"Well, I would like to see it please," Kate said as she set her teacup down and stood up from her chair.

"Right now?" Beth asked, sounding startled.

"Yes."

"I'm not sure that your husband would approve."

"My husband told me that I am in charge of whatever I'd like to be in charge of here in my home, and I say that it's fine."

Beth set her cup down as well and stood up to join Kate. She wasn't about to argue with her employer's wife.

As Beth led Kate through the kitchen and towards the wing of rooms at the back of the house, Kate could smell something delicious cooking on the stove.

"What is that you're making there?" she asked the cook.

"Bird stew," replied the elderly woman with a kind face.

Something about the woman's voice gave Kate an apprehensive feeling again and she rushed ahead to catch back up with Beth.

"Here it is," Beth said.

She waved Kate forward towards the short hallway with bedrooms lining either side.

"There aren't enough rooms," Kate noted.

She counted six bedroom doors, but knew her husband's staff vastly outnumbered that.

"We share," Beth said.

"Which one is yours?" Kate asked.

"Come," Beth said as she led her down the hallway. "I'll show you."

Beth's room was sparse and quaint, but it had all of the essentials one would need, including a few pleasant decorations. There were four beds in the room, meaning that Beth had three roommates. Kate assumed they were all single-sex rooms.

"Where is Isaac's room?" she asked.

She wasn't sure what made her ask, but she wanted to see where Isaac stayed.

"Oh, he doesn't have a room here," Beth replied.

"What? Why not? Where does he sleep?"

"Somewhere outside the main house, I'm not really sure where. I think he may have his own small cottage on the property."

It seemed reasonable to Kate that Isaac might have his own place to stay, after all, of all the servants, he had been in service to Ford's family the longest. But it was a bit curious that no one knew where his dwelling was. Perhaps it was by the beautiful garden that he seemed to love so much. She would have to ask Ford about it. Speaking of Ford, Kate realised that she hadn't seen him yet today and that she had been rather punitive towards him last night.

When she finally found Ford, he was sitting in his study busily working on ledgers and invoices. He looked up and set his pen down when Kate walked in.

"Hello," she said.

She moved closer to his desk and sat down in one of the chairs beside it.

The study was visibly intended for more than one person to work in, as was apparent by the several chairs that surrounded both the desk and the corners of the room.

"Kate," he said as he attempted a smile. "I'm glad to see you here. I wasn't sure how long your anger at me would last."

She sighed and reached for his hand, which he wrapped around her fingers on the top of his desk.

"I'm sorry," she said. "I don't like being upset with you."

"I'm not much of a fan of it either," Ford joked.

Kate laughed. She loved him, she truly did. But she still wanted a more believable answer from him than the ones he had been giving her.

"Can you tell me what you were really doing in the library?" she asked.

She hoped that maybe he would give her an answer that made sense so that she could move on from her over-thinking.

"I was honestly just reading," he said.

"When did you get back from your business in town?" she asked.

"What business?"

Kate tilted her head to the side and furrowed her brow.

"You said that you had to go into town for business yesterday," she said. "But then in the library, you told me that you had got back early and that is why you went into the library to read. So, I was just wondering when, exactly, you had got back."

"Oh," Ford said, rubbing his temple as if he had suddenly forgotten having gone into town at all. "I guess I don't remember. I'm sorry, my love."

Kate had a nagging worry that maybe her husband was working too hard and that his mind was going fuzzy due to a lack of rest. Then she remembered something else she had wanted to ask him about.

"Where does Isaac stay?" she asked.

"That's a peculiar question," Ford said. "Why do you want to know?"

"Beth showed me the servant's quarters and Isaac didn't have a room there. It made me curious about where he stays when he's not busy working for you."

"I think he stays somewhere on the grounds."

"That's a very vague answer," Kate said. "Don't

you want to know where your staff are staying on your own property?"

"Of course, I do," Ford answered. "And I do know where Isaac stays, I just can't remember it right this second."

Kate felt bad for giving him an interrogation. After all, he still hadn't given her any hard reason to mistrust him. She so desperately wanted to feel close to her new husband again.

"No more separate bedrooms," she blurted out.

"What?"

"I want you and I to stay in the same bedroom."

"I'm sorry Kate, but I've already told you how I feel about that. You and I both need our own space."

"But we're married!" she appealed to him. "How are we supposed to have sex if we aren't even sharing a bed?"

Ford's eyes flashed and a grin grew across his face.

"Is that what this is about? You need your husband to satisfy you? Oh Kate, I'm sorry that I've been so neglectful. I should have been more attentive to your needs. Trust me, I have those same needs as well."

Kate was about to tell him that sexual appetite had absolutely nothing to do with it, but she stopped herself when she saw that this might be a good way to get Ford to budge on the ridiculous idea of separate bedrooms.

"I will come to your room tonight, my love," he said as he smiled. "And we will be together."

Kate smiled at the "together" part. That was all she really wanted anyway. She didn't care whose room they were in, as long as they were together.

The evening passed quickly, mostly due to the excitement Kate felt about Ford staying in her bedroom with her tonight. They talked pleasantly over dinner, and he wasn't nearly as upset about the new table arrangement as she had thought he would be. In fact, it seemed as though he liked the smaller, more intimate setting better than the long table too. After dinner, Ford went to tie-up some loose ends for work in his study, and Kate went to her room. She had expected him to be longer than he was, but apparently Ford was excited about spending the evening with her too, because he was knocking on her door in no time.

When she opened the door, Ford's jaw dropped. Kate had already changed into one of her silkiest nightgowns, which clung to her body in all the right places. Regardless of what kind of man he was, whether it be a businessman or newlywed husband; he was still a man. And as such, he had desires like any other man. Kate smiled when she saw the look of desire on his face.

"You are so beautiful," he said.

He stepped inside and took Kate's hand. She blushed and walked with him over to the bed. It was strange that they'd been in this house for so many days since their wedding day and had yet to be intimate. Kate sat down on the edge of the bed as Ford stood before her. After a moment, he leaned down to kiss her. The feeling of his warm lips against hers seemed to dissolve all of her worries instantly. She pulled him towards her, and he followed her lead, climbing down on top of her as she laid her back down against the bed.

"I do love you Kate," he said as he kissed her and wrapped his arms around her.

"I love you too," she smiled.

This was all that she had wanted; just to know that she wasn't alone in this new life and that her husband loved her. And for a little while, she could forget about all the things that went bump in the night and raised the endings of her nerves.

After a satiating bout of lovemaking, Kate rested against Ford's shoulder in the bed and pulled the sheet over her. She rested her head against him and listened to his steady heartbeat. She traced her fingers over his chest and thought about how handsome he was, and what an exquisite lover he was too. She was lucky, even if there were some things that weren't exactly as she had hoped they would be. Surely all married couples had things to work through, and by staying here with her tonight, Ford had shown that he really was devoted to making it work between them.

"What shall we do tomorrow?" she asked, sleepily.

"I have a bit of work to take care of in the morning," he answered.

"You always have work," Kate sighed.

"Yes, that is true, but it is only to maintain a good life for us. Besides, it won't take me long."

"That's what you said the last time."

She wished she hadn't said it, because she was immediately reminded of the fact that it hadn't taken Ford long to finish his work the last time, and that instead he was hiding in the library that was restricted from her. She pushed the thoughts away and focused on more pleasant things, like the two of them being there together and the wonderful sex they had just had.

Ford didn't say anything else after that and as she nuzzled against the rise and fall of his chest – her hand in his and their legs intertwined – she fell asleep. It was the best night of sleep that she had experienced since coming to the house; no nightmares, no tossing and turning, just sleep. At one point in the night, she felt Ford turn over, and when he did, she turned over herself and wrapped the cosy blanket around her shoulders. She had fallen asleep with the delightful thought of waking up in her husband's arms and having Beth bring them both steaming cups of coffee in bed when the morning arrived. But when the morning did arrive, Kate was unpleasantly surprised to see that Ford was no longer there beside her. She sat up in bed and realised that what she had thought was simply Ford turning over in bed during the night, was actually him leaving. He hadn't stayed the night with her, he had got up and left as soon as she had fallen asleep.

Chapter Ten

A t breakfast, Ford looked exhausted, as if he hadn't slept a wink all night. Kate sipped her coffee and looked at him from across the table. Dark circles sagged under his eyes and he looked confused when she asked him about why he had left her bedroom during the night.

Instead of being angry with him, Kate was empathetic. Perhaps he was just working too hard. After all, it seemed as though he had been working nonstop since they'd arrived at the island together. Maybe he just needed to get some rest. When his coffee cup ran low, Kate picked it up to go and refill it for him in the kitchen.

"There's no need for you to do that," he said. "One of the staff will be around shortly with fresh coffee."

"Please, let me," Kate said. "You are my husband, and I can see that you'd like some more. Let me do something for you as you have done so much for me."

She got up and gave him a small kiss before she went to find more coffee from the servers.

Moments after she had gone, Isaac appeared with a fresh pot of coffee, ready to refill both of their cups. When he saw that Ford's cup was missing, he fetched another cup from the cabinet and placed it on the table. Then he sat down in Kate's seat and placed the pot down between the two of them.

When Kate returned with Ford's refilled cup, she was shocked to find Ford standing beside the table, pouring the steaming coffee into the cup which sat on the table in front of where Isaac was seated.

"Isaac?" she said as she walked closer to the men.

"Forgive me," Isaac said as he stood up from her seat. "I was just talking with your husband for a moment."

Kate looked at Ford, who had stopped pouring the coffee and looked around at the table as though he couldn't remember what he had been doing. He smiled at Kate and then sat back down as she handed him his fresh cup. Isaac quickly took the pot with him and left the room, leaving Kate with the filled cup that Ford had poured. It had almost appeared as if Ford had been serving Isaac. Kate knew how obviously ridiculous that was – too ridiculous to even mention to her husband. But she could not dismiss the fact that one of Ford's servants had taken her seat at the table. That seemed like something that should have bothered Ford too, but instead he seemed not to have even noticed it.

Once Ford had gone to his study to begin his work for the day, Kate began to feel claustrophobic even in the ginormous house. She wanted to go out, anywhere that wasn't inside. She asked Beth if she wanted to take a small trip to one of the nearby farmer's markets with her and, since it was ok with Ford, Beth agreed. Ford seemed to think that an outing would be good for lifting his wife's spirits. He loaded Kate up with some cash and arranged for their transportation. Kate was grateful that her husband seemed a bit less controlling than he had previously.

At the market, Kate was in heaven. The sights of brightly coloured fruits and vegetables, and the smells of fresh breads and cheeses were exactly what she needed. There were other things at the market too; some local artisan goods. She picked up a little treat to take back to Ford. Just as they were about to leave and head back to the house, Kate spotted a little table that had bags of fresh coffee beans displayed on it.

"Oh, I want to look here before we go," she told Beth as she tugged the servant's coat sleeve to pull her along.

"I don't think we should," Beth said.

"Why ever not?"

"Because that woman is quite strange," Beth answered, pointing at the woman sitting in a chair behind the table covered with coffees.

"Who cares?" Kate persisted. "We aren't bringing her home with us, just looking at what she has for sale. Besides, I would like to have some fresh flavours of coffee at the house."

Beth followed along warily as Kate went up to the table and greeted the woman there. As Kate picked out several bags of coffee, the woman looked at her with a wrinkled brow.

"Aren't you the woman who moved into that big house with Mr Billson?"

"Yes," Kate answered politely.

She handed her selection of coffees to the woman. The woman took her payment and started putting the coffees into a bag for her to carry them all.

"I'm sorry that you have to live in that house," she said to Kate. "You seem like a nice girl. It's a shame really."

"What do you mean?" Kate frowned.

"Don't listen to her," Beth said. "She's batty."

The woman laughed.

"See?" Beth said. "Just like I told you, she's crazy."

"I'm not laughing because I'm crazy," the woman said. "I'm laughing because you are. Living in that house, and all the while knowing that you should have abandoned it years ago. You're the crazy one. You could have just as easily got a job here in town instead of staying with that dreadful man."

"Hey!" Kate said defensively. "That's my husband you're talking about."

The woman looked at her in confusion for a moment and then laughed again.

"No dear," she said. "I'm not talking about Mr Billson. I'm talking about the original owner of that estate."

"You should keep your mouth shut," Beth snapped at the woman. "That was hundreds of years ago, and unless you were around then, you don't know anything about it."

"I know what I've heard," the woman persisted.

"And what is it that you've heard?" Kate asked.

"That your husband's mansion is haunted, and that it's been haunted for hundreds of years."

"Haunted?!" Kate exclaimed, suddenly feeling sick to her stomach.

"The original owner was a kindly old man, I heard. Kept to himself after his wife passed – mostly just read books, drank tea, and enjoyed his gardens. His wife was said to be a nice woman who he loved dearly. When she died, he stayed in their home alone, some say because it made him feel like he was still close to her."

"What happened to him?" Kate asked.

"Turns out, his wife had had an affair with one of the townsfolk. The old man found out and invited the other man over to the mansion for tea. He told him that it would serve them both to make peace with each other, for the sake of his wife. But when the man went to the old house, her husband murdered him. Stabbed him to death and wrapped him in a tablecloth before throwing him into deep water."

An image of the bloodied white tablecloth came to the forefront of Kate's mind and she felt as if her throat was constricting.

"When the old man eventually died in his bed from old age, other members of his family moved into the house. Generation after generation claimed that strange things went on while they lived there. Some couldn't even stand to stay there and quickly left."

"What kind of strange things?" Kate asked.

"Doors opening and closing, furniture moving itself, images of things that would appear and disappear, and the feeling that they were being watched."

Kate shuddered.

"Are you ok?" Beth asked her.

"Yeah," Kate lied. "I'm fine."

"From the looks of you," the woman said to Kate. "I'd go so far as to say you've seen some of that stuff yourself, haven't you?"

"Of course she hasn't," Beth interceded. "She's not crazy like you are. Now package up that coffee and let us leave."

The woman nodded her head in compliance and handed Kate the bag of coffee. When Kate reached for it, the woman grabbed her hand.

"You be careful in there," she said.

Beth pulled Kate alongside her as the two of them left the market to return home.

Chapter Eleven

Later in the evening, when Kate told her husband about what the woman at the market had said, he was back to his caring and devoted self. He worked hard to reassure Kate that the woman was simply crazy just like Beth had said.

"But there have been so many strange things that have occurred since I arrived here," Kate said, still not sure what to believe.

"There are always strange things in houses that are hundreds of years old," Ford replied. "But that certainly does not mean that the house is haunted."

He seemed to look a little less tired now. Perhaps he'd just needed to catch up on his work in order to be less stressed. Kate decided to take a chance at asking him why he'd left her bed during the middle of the night.

"Why did you leave after we'd made love?" she asked.

Ford looked slightly embarrassed for a moment, but then regained his composure.

"I just needed to get a few things done," he answered.

"In the middle of the night?"

"I think so."

"So, it wasn't because you didn't want to stay with me?" she asked.

"Oh, no. No. Of course not, my love, don't be silly," Ford said, shaking his head.

"Were you able to finish all your work today?" she asked.

"Yes."

"Good," Kate said. "Then you should have no trouble staying in the bed with me tonight."

Before Ford had a chance to argue with her about it, Kate put her mouth on his and kissed him. She reached her hand into his trousers and felt him draw his arms around her. When she stood up, he followed.

This time, after they had made love, she asked him point-blank about what he would do.

"Will you leave me again tonight?" she demanded to know. "I don't want you to. I want you to stay here with me. It's not at all natural for a husband and wife not to share a bed. Promise me that you'll stay the night here."

She felt the rise and fall of Ford's deep sigh before he answered.

"Alright," he said. "I promise."

"Good," Kate smiled with satisfaction. "I only really ever slept well that one night that you were there beside me."

"How come?" Ford asked.

She could see the small frown on his mouth as his lips turned downwards at the edges. She knew that he cared for her and he truly didn't like seeing her unhappy or ill at ease.

"Every time I close my eyes, I see that damned crow," Kate answered.

"It's just a bird, my love. It can't hurt you. Perhaps you should try to think of a different kind of bird before you fall asleep. Maybe that little trick will chase the crow from your dreams."

Kate liked the idea, almost as much as she liked the fact that Ford would stay by her side through the night. She chose to envision a cardinal – such a pretty bird, so colourful and bright; the complete opposite of the black crow. She pictured a beautiful red cardinal in her mind as she closed her eyes.

At the beginning of her deep sleep, it seemed to work. Kate dreamt of walking along the garden path hand-in-hand with Ford as the white snow fell softly around them. Ahead of them on the ground, she saw a cardinal standing out brilliantly against the backdrop of the snow. As they walked closer to the bird, it opened its mouth and made a dreadful cawing sound. Ford started to laugh, and she found it quite rude. Just as they had almost reached the cardinal, she watched as the bird suddenly looked nothing like a cardinal anymore, but instead a crow whose feathers had been soaked with a bright red blood. The colour dripped off the tips of its wings and beak, and onto the blanket of white snow beneath it. She tried to turn and run, but Ford still had hold of her hand and he was rooted firmly in place, still laughing at an increasing volume. She cried to him, but his laughter continued. At the moment right before her eyes shot open, the bloodied crow flew up at her face. The dream felt so real that she could feel the wet drops of blood spray against her cheeks.

When she awoke, her hands reflexively wiped her face. And when she felt a wetness at her fingertips, she panicked until she brought her hands into focus and could see that the wetness was from her tears and not from the blood in her nightmare.

She turned to reach for Ford, but he was gone.

Chapter Twelve

There was no quenching Kate's thirst for answers when the first beam of morning light shone through the window. After searching the entire estate for Ford without success, she decided instead, that she would take a look inside his bedroom. She knew where it was located, but out of respect for her husband's wishes, she had never dared to venture inside. Now, having been abandoned in her bed during the night once again, she could see no point in exacerbating her anxieties further and instead sought to discover the truth about her husband once and for all.

She had expected the door to Ford's bedroom to be locked, but all it took was a small turn of the handle for it to pop open. Ford was not in the room, but what she saw was so disturbing that it took her breath away. The room was stark and grey, empty of all the personal paraphernalia that one might have in a bedroom. The only things that covered all of the empty space were the dozens of crude sketches of an image that haunted Kate, even in her dreams. The walls were papered with sheets filled with the charcoal-drawn lines of the crow.

Fear crept up her spine as Kate walked further into Ford's bedroom. Each of the drawings seemed to stare at her from off the paper, and each looked as though it had been drawn in a feverish fit of delusion. This couldn't possibly have been Ford's doing. It was simply not something that he would do. It went against everything that Kate knew about him. She looked around the room in panic until something on the side of the bed caught her attention. When she picked it up, she saw that it was something familiar to her, something she had seen before. Kate picked up the gold ring and turned it over in her hand. She recognised the piece of jewellery as the same one that had been on Isaac's finger. But why in the world would it be here in Ford's bedroom?

Kate hastily shoved the ring in her pocket and went to take a closer look at the drawings on the walls. Nubs of broken charcoal sticks crunched beneath her feet as she walked. Judging by all of the scattered drawing tools on the floor, whoever had made the drawings (and she still hoped to God that it wasn't Ford) must have been in either a hurry or a frenzy. Kate reached for one of the drawings; a large piece of white paper with the image of a crow in mid-flight. The head of the creature was pitch-black and thick with charcoal, and the lines led outwards towards smudged outstretched wings that seemed to fade off the page. When Kate touched the edge of the paper, a shot of coldness ran through her, making her veins feel as if they had been infused with ice instead of warm blood.

"What kind of room is this?" she shouted aloud even though no one was there to answer her. "What kind of man have I married?"

In terror, she began to run from the room, unsure of whether she should seek out her husband further or beg Beth to help her get away from here and back to her old life – whatever that would look like now. As it happened though, Kate came to a full stop as soon as her feet stepped back into the hallway, because there, on the floor in front of her, was the crow.

Despite its size standing about as tall as just above her ankles, the crow had a commanding and eerie presence that consumed the entire corridor. It stared at her with demanding eyes that seemed to have both nothing and everything behind them. Kate took off her shoe and threw it at the bird. Even though her aim was bad, it nearly struck it on the back. Unfazed, the crow simply stepped forward, avoided the blow, and walked closer towards Kate. She thought birds were supposed to hop on their small feet, but instead this one walked as if it had the weight of a man. With its beak curved upwards at the edges, it almost looked like the crow was smiling. It was the kind of smile that a circus clown would use to over-exaggerate its mouth.

It's only a bird, Kate thought. Surely, she could just run past it. But when she tried, the crow became wildly aggressive. It flew at her as she covered her face. It pecked at her arms and shoulders and pulled strands of hair from her head. The bird's cawing sounds rang through the old house like a war cry and Kate felt hopeless that anyone would come to help her. Even though she felt her feet running down the hallway, every time she darted her eyes above her arms, it seemed that she had got disoriented and had turned around in the hallway; she was right back where she had started, standing just outside Ford's bedroom door. She screamed and in all of her panic, she tried to tell herself that this was probably just another one of her disturbing nightmares. But when she felt the blood from the crow's assault dripping down her forehead, she could tell that it wasn't a dream at all, not this time.

She heard the sound of someone coming, and then saw the footsteps of a man below her arms (she still had them raised so that they were covering her face). As soon as a hand reached out to take her by the shoulder, the crow flew off. Where it went, she had no idea, since all of the windows were closed. When Kate lowered her hands and opened her eyes, it was Isaac who stood before her.

"My goodness," he said, with a look of odd concern. "Are you alright, Kate?"

She pushed his arm away and took a few steps back from him.

"Did you see the crow?" she asked.

She was afraid that yet again she would be the only one in the house claiming to have seen the odd occurrences.

"Yes, of course I saw the crow. How could I not have? It seems to have been attacking you."

Kate sighed with relief. But then she remembered what she had seen in Ford's bedroom, and Isaac's ring that was tucked inside of her pocket.

"Where is my husband?" she shouted.

"I'm sorry to say that he went into town on a business trip. He should be back by dinnertime. Let me help you get cleaned up."

"No," Kate hollered. "Don't you come near me."

Isaac smiled. It sent the same chill up Kate's spine as it had done before in the library.

"Kate," he said. "My dear, whatever is the matter with you?"

"What are all of those drawings in Ford's bedroom?" she said as she pointed behind her into the room. "Why are his walls covered with drawings of the bird that just attacked me?"

Isaac walked past Kate and looked into the room. When he turned around, he looked completely indifferent.

"Mr Billson is an appreciator of the arts. He sometimes likes to dabble in sketching."

Kate could tell that he was lying.

"Why are they all crows?" she demanded.

"The crow is Mr Billson's family crest. It's part of your husband's ancestry which dates back hundreds of years to his oldest relatives."

"Why did you not tell me that before?" she said.

"You never asked."

None of this sounded right to Kate. All of it seemed crazy. She stood in the hall trying to think as Isaac stared at her and waited to see what she would do.

"Where do you sleep, Isaac?" she asked as her thoughts began to pull together.

"Pardon me?" he said.

"Where," Kate spoke slower and louder the second time she asked. "Do you sleep?"

"Well, I hardly think that should be any concern of yours," he smiled. "But I have a little cottage shed by the garden – the one with all the wildflowers that I showed to you."

"I didn't see any shed there."

"Then perhaps you were not looking in the right direction," Isaac shrugged.

Kate dug into her pocket and pulled out the gold ring.

"This is your ring. I saw it on your hand previously. I just found it in my husband's bedroom. What was it doing in there?"

Isaac held out his hand to take the ring from her, but Kate closed her fingers around it. For a moment, a look of anger grew on his face, which he quickly subsided and replaced with a smile.

"Wonderful," he said pleasantly. "I thought I had lost my ring. I reported it missing to Mr Billson after I had done some gardening around the estate.

Your husband must have found it for me, for which I am exceptionally grateful. That ring means a great deal to me, if I could please have it back?"

Isaac extended his hand out again. Kate knew once more that he was lying, but there was nothing that she could do to prove it. She had no evidence with which to accuse him of being dishonest. She reluctantly opened her fingers and gave Isaac his ring back.

"Thank you," he said as he placed the ring on his wedding finger. "Now, if I may, I would like to help you get cleaned up before your husband returns. He's been working so much lately that it would be a shame to cause him further stress. I know that his main concern always lies with your wellbeing."

There was nothing else that Kate could do. She had nothing to accuse Isaac of besides coming to her aid. She was already skating on thin ice. Her behaviour was such that Ford might already think of her as crazy. But honestly, maybe it was Ford who was crazy himself. Her head was spinning, and she was feeling scared, and confused, and unwell. So, she allowed Isaac to put his arm around her waist and help her walk towards the living room in order to tend to her cuts and scratches.

Once he had her seated, Isaac went to fetch some

antiseptic and bandages. It was not him who returned though, instead it was Beth who came into the room with the first aid supplies.

"What happened to you?" she asked.

She rushed over and began wiping Kate's forehead with a wet cloth.

"I don't know," Kate answered.

"Isaac said that a crow attacked you! How did the bird get into the house?"

"I don't know," Kate said again. "Beth, have you ever been inside of my husband's bedroom?"

"Of course not!" she said, taken aback. "Why in the world would you ask me if I'd been in your husband's bedroom? I have a man of my own who I am seeing."

"I didn't mean it like that," Kate said, shaking her head. "I just wondered if you had ever seen inside of the room."

"No. Why do you ask?"

"I was just wondering."

Once Kate was cleaned up and had sat with a cup of tea for a moment to try and relax, she heard Ford come into the house. Isaac had told him of the incident and naturally, it made him very worried. He moved as quickly as he could to be by her side.

"Darling," he fussed over her. "I am so sorry to hear of what happened. I have ordered Isaac to double-check all of the windows in the house to make sure they are closed. There must have been an open window somewhere which allowed the rabid bird to get inside."

"Birds cannot be rabid, I don't think," Kate said as she stared vacantly at her husband. "May I ask you something, Ford?"

"Of course, what is it?"

"Why do we sleep apart? And why do you always go back to your separate bedroom, which I have never been invited into?"

"I've told you," he answered. "I believe it's important for us to each have our own space."

"And it has nothing to do with the fact that you might be hiding something from me?"

"Hiding?" Ford asked, sounding surprised at the allegation. "What would I possibly be hiding from you?"

"I have seen your room, dear husband. I have seen all of the madness that covers the walls of it.

Explain yourself please."

Ford looked cornered and embarrassed. Then he startled Kate by laughing a bit under his breath.

"It is true, there is a bit of madness on the walls of my bedroom. Isaac has been giving me art lessons, something at which I am not talented but would like to learn. My work leaves so little time for pleasures such as the creation of art, and I know I am a fool to pursue such a trivial thing. But Isaac has been kind enough to indulge me with some lessons. I was embarrassed to tell you for fear that you would think of me as silly."

Kate was surprised to hear this confession from her husband. She also wasn't sure whether to believe it.

"Why are all the drawings of a crow? The same crow that keeps haunting me?"

"Simply because it is a common bird to see around here and therefore was the most accessible model for our drawing lessons. There is no other reason," Ford assured her.

Kate shook her head. She felt as if her sanity was slipping away.

Ford bid the servants to begin with the dinner preparations. He attentively stayed by Kate's side for the rest of the evening. They talked of various things and spent some moments in silence, in which Kate replayed – in her mind – the events from the day and struggled to make any sense of them still.

Just before they parted ways for bed, Kate asked her husband about the gold ring.

"Isaac was very pleased that you found his ring," she said. "He was happy to have it returned."

"What ring?" Ford asked.

Chapter Thirteen

That evening, as Beth was helping to fold down the bed sheets and light a peaceful candle in Kate's bedroom, Kate pulled her aside.

"You've worked here a long time," Kate said to her. "Long enough to be familiar with the routines of the house."

"Yes, I have," Beth answered.

"Tell me, why do you think my husband doesn't want to stay in the same room as me?"

Beth looked uncomfortable as she continued to busy herself with things around the room.

"Beth, please," Kate begged.

Beth stopped her work and looked as though she felt sorry for Kate. She sat down on the side of the bed next to her and sighed.

"I think Mr Billson has the separate bedroom arrangement for your protection."

"My protection?" Kate asked, stunned. "What is it that he is protecting me from?"

"Himself."

Kate's eyes grew wide with fear. Could it be possible that all of her deepest worries and anxieties were true?

"Beth, you have to explain to me what you mean," Kate said, getting increasingly upset.

"Mr Billson has never had anyone else in this house with him. For as long as I've known him, he's never been with another woman. When he came back from the trip that he had met you on, he was the happiest I have ever seen him. He truly loves you, Kate."

That made Kate smile.

"But there are rumours about this house," Beth continued. "And whether they are true or not, I don't think he is willing to risk it, not with you."

"Rumours like the ones that the woman at the market was talking about?"

"Yes," Beth answered, bowing her head in defeat.

"But I thought you said she was crazy and that none of that was true."

"That woman is crazy," Beth nodded. "But parts of the rumours are truer than others."

"Which parts?" Kate asked.

"The original owner who she spoke of, the old man; he lived in this house for a long time after his wife's death before he met with his own end. After murdering his wife's lover, it has been said that he went rather mad himself."

"Well, obviously he was mad," Kate said. "He did, after all, kill someone."

"I don't know about that," Beth said, still believing some of the rumours to be fictional. "But apparently he was so bitter about his dead wife's indiscretions, that he cursed the house against any man and woman who would ever share a bed together through the night."

"So, the house is haunted then?" Kate asked, looking for something to go on which would at least begin to explain things.

"I don't believe in haunted houses," Beth said. "But it's possible that your husband does."

Kate's head was spinning. It was becoming

increasingly difficult to sort out what was real and true, and what wasn't. Each time she pictured Ford in her head, she wasn't sure whether to picture him as the hero or the villain. And each time she thought about Isaac, she became increasingly distraught.

Beth was getting ready to leave the room. She was about to bid Kate goodnight.

"Tell me," Kate asked. "What are your feelings about Isaac?"

"Isaac?" Beth said. "I think he is a strange old man, but a harmless one at that. He's been in your husband's service for longer than anyone, and even longer than that. Goodnight Kate."

Kate's sleep was disturbed during the night. She tossed and turned and woke in a cold sweat to the sight of a deep fog lingering in her bedroom, and her windows thrown open. She got up from the bed and went to close the windows, thinking that the fog would then dissipate, but when it remained, she felt as though she was still stuck in her dreams. Shadows lurked around the edges of the room and taunted her with their shapes that resembled the beaks and tails of crows.

She wasn't sure whether she was awake, or still asleep. But even when she crawled back into her bed to try and close her eyes again, she seemed to be stuck in some sort of consciousness limbo. When she was finally able to fall back into sleep, all of the bits and pieces of recent events hurled themselves together into a formidable nightmare. Instead of one crow, she saw thousands and they all seemed to have a face which looked like Isaac's. Beth and the woman from the market walked together in her dream, holding hands and wading into the sea until they seemed to become one. The sea itself turned a sickly shade of red that reminded her of dried blood, and the vines in the garden began to encroach into the house as if they meant to strangle it from the inside out.

The only thing in Kate's nightmare that didn't terrify her, was Ford. Ford stood at the edge of her dream, as if he was urging her to go with him. When Kate reached her hand out towards him and was almost about to feel his touch, she awoke.

She looked around her room in fear, but there was nothing there; no crows, no servants, and no fog hovering in her room. The windows were all closed and the shadows that she had seen creeping about were no longer there. Kate was fairly sure that she was awake now, and she was also fairly sure that she wanted to be near her husband and not back in her bed alone. So, she walked out of her room and down the hall towards Ford's bedroom.

When she pushed open the door to his room, she saw him there in his bed sleeping. There was a single, tall candle in the room which cast a soft glow of light over everything. Although the sketches of crows adorning the walls were still unsettling, Kate was not as creeped-out by them as she had been before. Either she was becoming more brave, or less wary of her husband. She wasn't sure which of those two things it was yet.

She walked over to Ford's bed and crawled in beside him. When Ford felt her there, he woke and opened his eyes.

"Kate!" he said in surprise. "What are you doing here?"

"I cannot sleep without you tonight," she said as she looked at him with pleading eyes.

"Ok," he said. "Come, I will go back to your bedroom with you."

Kate pulled him back towards her when he tried to sit up.

"No," she said. "I will stay in here with you tonight. That way, I know that you won't leave me once I'm asleep."

Ford looked as though he was tired and torn, as if he was desperately trying to do the right thing by his wife but was finding it increasingly difficult.

"Kate," he said. "You can't stay in here."

She gently pushed his chest down so that his back was flat against the bed. She crawled on top of him and cradled his body between her thighs.

"Yes," she said. "I can."

Before Ford had a chance to argue with her further, Kate bent over and began to kiss him. This time, less soft and less reserved than before. She pushed her tongue into his mouth. Ford was overwhelmed by her and couldn't resist the sensual nature of his wife straddled over him. He pulled the sheets out from between them and Kate lifted her nightgown. She pulled her husband inside of her as he moaned with pleasure and succumbed to his desire for her.

As the two of them enjoyed a passion that stoked hotter than it ever had before, the old house seemed to heave in disagreement. The wind whipped against the windows outside. The candle flickered even though all the windows in the bedroom were closed tight. The floorboards creaked and the frame of the old house groaned, despite the fact that no one was walking about it. Even the air in the old house seemed heavy with unsettled emotion. Kate and Ford noticed none of it, not even the cawing of the crow coming from the gardens outside. They were too indulged in their lovemaking to pay it any attention. When the final moment drew near, there was a pained howl that rose up through the house and shook the very foundation.

Ford cradled Kate in his arms and whispered to her how much he loved her. Clouded by his body's fatigue and his enchantment with his wife, he forgot about trying to shoo her back into her own room and fell asleep with her in his bed.

Kate felt safe and appeased in her husband's bed. She was confident that this time, she would wake up with his body next to hers. She closed her eyes and allowed herself to fall into a restful sleep. Neither of them dreamt any more that night.

Meanwhile, off in the servant's quarters, Beth woke troubled from her sleep. The sounds of the house had invaded her peaceful slumber. She sat up in her bed trembling and afraid. She looked around at the other women who shared the room with her. They were all fast off with no trouble to be seen. She went to the kitchen to get a glass of water. When she looked out of the window and saw Isaac standing in the middle of the garden staring back at her, the glass slipped from her fingers and fell to the floor, shattering next to her bare feet. She looked down momentarily at the shards of glass and then back up again to look out of the window at Isaac. He was no longer there.

Beth convinced herself that she must have dreamt that she'd seen Isaac. After all, she hadn't been fully awake when entering the kitchen and was probably still hazy. After she'd cleaned up the broken glass, she went back to bed. She, like everyone else in the old house, knew how easy it was to give in to an overactive imagination and let the middle-of-the-night sights and sounds play tricks on the mind. She chuckled at herself and brushed off her fears as she closed her eyes and went back to sleep.

Chapter Fourteen

In the morning, all was well just as Kate had hoped it would be. She woke up to Ford still right beside her. Once the two of them had got moving for the day, they went to enjoy a nice breakfast together. Ford had agreed to take the day off from work so that he and Kate could spend it together, which delighted her tremendously.

Somewhere in the midst of their conversations, Kate brought up the subject of the restricted library again. She asked Ford why she couldn't go inside the room to choose a book to read for the following day when he would be working in the study for most of the time. On this occasion when she asked about it, Ford didn't seem to have a solid answer as to why she couldn't do as she was asking. So, he agreed that the next morning, she could enter the library to select a book to read for her pleasure. Kate was content and things seemed to be much more at ease – both between the two of them and overall in the house.

That afternoon, they enjoyed a beautiful picnic out on the grounds. Beth had brought along a blanket for them and a most delicious spread of charcuterie, along with a bottle of wine that revealed the most beautiful aroma when Ford popped it open. Beth and two of the other servant women enjoyed their own lunch at a slight distance, just in case Kate and Ford needed anything else.

"This is truly a wonderful day," Kate smiled.

She and Ford clinked their long-stemmed glasses together.

"I'm glad that you're happy," he said.

He leaned forward to kiss her softly on the mouth before she took a sip of her wine.

"I am," Kate said. "In fact, I am so happy and so in love with you, that I think we should talk about starting a family."

"A family?" Ford's eyebrows raised.

"Yes. What do you think?"

"I… I think that…"

Before Ford had a chance to address Kate's

question in one way or another, Isaac swooped in like a bird of prey and interrupted their revelry.

"Excuse me sir," Isaac said, assertively.

"Isaac, what are you doing here?" Ford asked.

"My apologies, but some of your work partners have been calling to the house and there seems to be an issue that needs your attention. I hate to break up your picnic with Mrs Billson, but I believe you may want to make a trip into town."

Isaac glanced at Kate before looking back to receive Ford's answer.

"Kate, I'd like to continue this conversation with you when I return home," Ford said as he turned his focus towards her. "I promise that I won't be long."

"Ford…" Kate started to say.

She didn't want him to leave, not right now when everything was finally going so well.

"It's ok," he said as he smiled at her lovingly. "I'll be home by dinner, and we can resume this exact conversation then. You have my word."

There was something in his eyes that had changed, something that Kate found extremely comforting and trustworthy.

"Ok," she agreed.

After giving Kate a small kiss on the cheek, Ford got up and left with Isaac.

Beth and the other servants helped Kate to clear up the picnic and bring everything back to the house. Everything seemed to be heading towards the conclusion of a great day, even though the picnic had been interrupted. Isaac had taken Ford into the town to attend to whatever pressing business matter needed his attention, but Kate was looking forward to their dinner together later that evening.

As dinnertime approached, Kate searched through her wardrobe to find something beautiful to wear. She wanted to make the dinner date with her husband as enchanting as possible, and she wanted him to feel as much hope and joy about starting a family together as she did. The echoes of the unease she had felt here in the house still lingered slightly, but now that she and Ford seemed to have rekindled their strong affections, and he seemed much more supportive and attentive than he had before, Kate was sure that she had made the right choice and that Ford would remain by her side forever. She had always wanted to have a child. Besides, they had the means and she wasn't getting any younger.

She dressed and looked at herself in the mirror as

she ran a deep red lipstick over her lips. She was sure that Ford would find her irresistible tonight, and since she no longer had to worry about sleeping alone, her mind was at ease. At least, that is, until her husband didn't show up for dinner.

Kate sat at the table waiting while the servants brought her glass after glass of wine. When two hours had passed, and Ford still wasn't home, she began to worry. She called Beth to her and tried to bury the panic in her voice.

"He's not home," she said to Beth. "Isaac took him into town, and he promised that he would be home by dinnertime and he's not here. What has happened?"

Beth looked alarmed but tried to reassure Kate as much as she could.

"I'm sure that everything is fine," she said with a forced smile. "Perhaps they got delayed by something, or maybe a meeting ran late. I'm sure Mr Billson will be home soon. In the meantime, you shouldn't wait any longer for dinner. You need to eat."

Kate shook her head and waved her hand at Beth to dismiss her. She had no desire to eat. Her stomach was in knots and her mind was running rampant with a whole host of possible scenarios of what could have happened to Ford. None of them were good. She sat at the table and continued to drink the wine that the servants brought in until she was too tired for more. Her senses were too mumbled and numbed to keep herself from resting her head on the table in front of her.

After a while, she felt Beth tapping her on the shoulder.

"Kate," Beth said. "It's late. Let me help you to bed."

Had Kate been less inebriated, she might have thought to ask Beth what the time was. And she might have found out that it was two o'clock in the morning and that Ford still hadn't returned. But Kate was drunk and exhausted. She let Beth escort her to the bedroom. It wasn't until Beth had helped her change into her nightgown and was about to put her into her bed, that Kate seemed to snap into a mode of lucidity.

"No!" Kate said, as she waved her hands drunkenly in the air. "I don't want to sleep here. I will sleep in Ford's room tonight."

"As you wish," Beth said.

Against her better judgement, Beth escorted Kate to Ford's bedroom. Once the servant had blown out the candle and left the room, Kate dropped off to sleep on Ford's wide and empty bed. She thought she might have heard the cawing of crows around her as the sketches that graced the walls blew in an unnatural breeze, but she was too tired to think about it.

When Kate awoke, and saw that Ford still hadn't returned to her side, she began to panic yet again. Beth came in to bring the morning coffee and told Kate that Ford still hadn't returned from town and that neither had Isaac. Once again, she tried to assure her that they had probably got delayed on a business matter, but Kate just couldn't believe it. Something wasn't right. A feeling of dread came over her and she insisted that a few of the staff go into town to search for her husband. In the meantime, Beth advised Kate to find something to do to keep her mind busy and less worried.

Kate remembered that Ford had given her permission to visit the library to get a book to read. She figured that he wouldn't mind if she went there now. After all, if he had any idea how worried she was, he would probably *insist* that she visit the library to calm her nerves.

Once inside the library, a chill swept over Kate as she remembered the encounter she'd had the last time she was there. She didn't trust Isaac, and she was not happy that he was the one who was with her husband now.

The library was dimly lit and brimming with books. There was an oversized armchair to sit in and a little table with a lamp on it in the centre. Bookcases lined the room and they were so overly stuffed with books that it was difficult to work out how they were all organised. Kate wasn't even sure what kind of book she wanted to read – maybe a fantasy to take her mind away from focusing on Ford's return. Beth was probably right; Ford was probably just delayed and would be coming through the door at any moment. Kate figured that she would be better off losing her mind in a story rather than obsessively worrying herself.

She walked along the bookshelves, letting her fingers drag over the spines of the books as she perused their covers. Most of the books looked rather boring; historical accounts, biographies – all things that Kate had no interest in reading about. There didn't seem to be any fantasy novels anywhere. But then she saw a small section on one of the bottom shelves that housed books with interesting-looking bindings. The books were covered in leather with embossed titles and the edges of the pages were gilded with a dusky golden colour. They looked too special and too unique to be left on the bottom shelf of the bookcase. She picked one up to look at and was rather surprised by its title: *The Ancestry of the Billson Family.*

Thinking that it was probably the most interesting book in the library, Kate sat down with it in the armchair and cracked it open to begin reading. It was a very thick and large book and was filled with pages and pages of text, as well as with old black and white photographs. It was a complete anthology of Ford's family heritage, complete with family names and photographs dating back hundreds of years. When the lineage pre-dated the invention of the camera, there were sketches of the family members' likenesses on the pages instead. It was extremely interesting. The account carried on all the way through to Ford's parents, who were the most recent entry in the book. Even Ford himself had a photograph on one of the pages, taken from when he was a baby. At the very bottom of the last page was a notation in small print, directing the reader to the other volume of the anthology.

There were two books.

Kate set the book down on the table next to the lamp and went back to the shelf to see if she could find the second book. With luck, she did. The second book wasn't nearly as thick as the last one, but it seemed complete. She looked at the handwritten index in the front of the book and read over the names listed, all the way to the bottom of the list. At the very bottom, it listed the name, *I.*

Billson, original owner of the estate.

How intriguing, Kate thought. She was so curious to see the man who had all of the ever-present rumours concocted about him, that the books had served their purpose in helping her forget about Ford's absence. She skimmed through the pages of the book, stopping to read more thoroughly about the people that seemed interesting to her. Ford certainly had an interesting family line, and a wealthy one at that. It seemed that the old wealth in his family pre-dated even what he might have known about. As she reached the end of the book, the last page was dedicated to the original owner of the estate, *Isaac Billson*.

A cold shudder went through Kate's entire body. Surely that name was just a coincidence? It had to be! There were many people in the world named Isaac, and it couldn't possibly be the same man she knew since this would have been several hundred years ago. She laughed at herself, knowing full-well that she was being ridiculous and letting her imagination get the better of her. She needed to stop letting the old servant creep her out so much. There was no picture of Isaac Billson for some reason, so when Kate finished reading about him, she went back to the shelf to see if there were any other volumes to read, which there were not. The other books on the shelf were more of the same boring historical non-fiction that lined the rest of the bookcases.

Just as she was getting ready to replace the ancestral anthologies that she had read, she noticed a yellowed piece of paper sticking out from beneath one of the other books on the bottom shelf. She tugged at the paper to pull it out. When she was able to see what was on it, she felt sick, as if she was going to pass out on the spot.

The paper was an old sketch, done in charcoal, featuring the exact likeness of the Isaac that she knew; the servant Isaac that was now somewhere in town supposedly with Ford.

At the bottom of the sketch there was a label, dated for approximately several hundred years in the past:

Isaac A. Billson, original owner of the estate. May he rest in peace eternally.

Chapter Fifteen

As Kate sat holding the picture of Isaac in her hands, the sound of beating wings came from above the bookcase. She looked up to see the crow sitting perched on the shelf and looking down at her.

"What beautiful creatures crows are, aren't they?"

Kate looked up to see Isaac standing in the doorway to the library.

"Where is my husband?" Kate demanded abruptly.

She stood up, still clenching onto the picture in her hand.

"He is working," Isaac answered her.

"Did you even take him into town yesterday?" she asked, backing slowly up against the library wall as far as she could.

"No. Mr Billson does most of his work here at the estate, for me."

"What kind of work does my husband do for you?" Kate asked, confused.

"Whatever I want him to do. Sometimes he tends to my gardens, sometimes he draws pictures of my friendly familiar," Isaac said, waving his hand up towards the crow.

"I don't think my husband would want to do anything for you. He's not a servant, you are," Kate said with as much confidence as she could muster.

Isaac laughed and the crow echoed his laughter with an eerie screech.

"He doesn't have much choice in the matter," Isaac said. "Most of the time he doesn't even know what he's doing. He's like a puppet. You could call it a privilege of having the family on my side."

"What family?"

"Come now, Kate. Surely, you mustn't be that daft. All of the ancestors you've been reading about in these books. They are all my family. And they support me, even from where they now rest."

Kate was sure this was insane. All of the people in those books had died long ago.

"You're dead!" she said as a feeling of sickness filled her stomach. "You died a long time ago, didn't you?"

"Yes."

"Why do you still remain here in this estate? Why not go on to your final resting place somewhere else?"

"We have unfinished business here," he said.

Kate finally understood now that the crow who had been stalking her this entire time, was indeed a friend of Isaac. Just as he had told her that day on the garden bench; the crow was a bridge between the land of the living and the land of the dead.

"You have no unfinished business with Ford. We haven't wronged you in any way."

"EVERYONE has wronged me!" Isaac shouted.

The crow became agitated and flew from the top of one bookcase to another.

"Everyone has betrayed me and cheated me of my home, and my love, and my life," Isaac continued. "Everyone in this family will suffer. And now, that includes you."

"No. It doesn't have to," Kate begged, not knowing what else to do. "You can just let us go and we will leave. You'll never have to see or hear from us again, I swear it."

"That's not true, Kate."

Isaac looked eerily creepier and more decrepit than before. His skin looked translucent and his eyes looked like miniature caves sitting on his face.

"Yes, yes, it is true," Kate insisted. "We will leave right away this very night. Just tell me where Ford is, and we will leave!"

"Don't think you can fool me. I heard you talking. I heard you say you wanted children. Do you really think that I would let this bloodline continue? No. It ends with your husband, and with you. Then my dear old house can finally return to its quiet and peaceful state without any further chance of intrusion."

Isaac started walking towards Kate as the crow flew down and circled above her head. She looked around the room in panic but there was no other way out except for the doorway – which was behind Isaac – and a large window in the side wall of the room that would lead to certain death due to the drop off the side.

Kate screamed, hoping that Ford would hear her, wherever he was. But instead of Ford coming to her rescue, Beth appeared at the door behind Isaac.

"What is going on in here?" she asked when she saw the terrified look on Kate's face. "Isaac, what are you doing? And what is that bird doing in here?"

Kate had no chance to warn her of what was happening before Isaac waved his hand towards the crow. It launched itself at Beth. The poor woman stumbled around in the library as she tried to swat the bird away without being able to see anything in front of her. As Beth neared the edge of the room and stumbled over her own feet, Kate cried for her to watch out for the window. But it was too late, Beth's body broke through the glass and hurled down towards the drop below.

The crow circled back into the room with a triumphant caw as Kate stood looking horrified at the murder of her one friend in the house.

"Are you going to kill me too?" she asked Isaac.

He smiled and she saw that his teeth looked rotten now and his jaw looked as though it was barely attached to the rest of his skull. How had she not seen this before; how had he been able to hide his appearance of death? Maybe Kate had been too distracted to notice. Perhaps it was the crow who had helped him, or perhaps it was this stupid house.

"Where's Ford? What have you done with him?!" Kate pleaded hysterically.

Isaac didn't answer her. He simply continued his

slow walk towards her as she slid against the wall with her palms pressed flat onto its cold surface. Tears started to stream down her face as she thought about how Ford could already be dead. She feared the strong possibility that she would be soon.

She stopped shuffling against the wall when she reached the same part of it that framed the broken window. There was nowhere else for her to run. The crow settled itself upon Isaac's shoulder as he drew closer to her. With every step that he took, his appearance deteriorated to look more and more ghastly, until at last, she was nearly too terrified to look at him.

Just as Kate thought she was about to meet with the same fate that Beth had, a hand reached from behind Isaac and grabbed the crow by its neck.

"Ford!" Kate shouted.

Her husband was now standing behind Isaac with the bird grasped solidly in his clutches.

Isaac spun around in shock. He saw the bird being choked between Ford's squeezing fingers and his eyes flared with rage. He mumbled a few strange words under his breath and then both he and the crow seemed to vanish into thin air, leaving Ford's empty, outstretched hands held up in front of him.

As startled as Ford was, he was only concerned about Kate. He ran towards her and embraced her in his arms.

"Are you alright?" he asked.

"Oh my God! I thought you were dead!" she cried as she buried her head against his chest.

"No, not dead, just tricked. Isaac was somehow able to get in my head. I'm not sure how, but somehow. I heard you calling for me and I snapped out of it. I found myself locked in the pantry and had to break the door down from the inside in order to get out. I'm not even sure how I got in there to begin with. The last thing I remembered was being at the picnic with you."

Kate raised her head up to look at him through tear-filled eyes.

"Ford, we have to get out of here right now!" she insisted. "He isn't among the living; Isaac will come back to get us."

"I agree," Ford said. "We need to leave."

They went together to their rooms and quickly grabbed only a few necessary possessions – Ford's wallet and a jacket for Kate – then they hurried out of the house.

Chapter Sixteen

Once they reached the town, Ford made arrangements for them to catch the next ferry out to anywhere, anywhere but here! As they waited in the car to board the ferry that would take them away from the island, Ford held Kate tightly in his arms and stroked her hair.

"I promise you that everything will be ok," he spoke to her softly. "We will get out of here and never look back. We'll start a new life somewhere else, anywhere you want to go. We'll start the family that you were trying to talk to me about. And we'll be happy. I promise you that, Kate. I love you."

She looked up at him and kissed him. None of this had been Ford's fault and she knew that now. As scared as she was from the whole ordeal, she was relieved that Ford was indeed the man she'd hoped him to be. At least they were together now –

although she wasn't quite convinced that a past a troubling as this would be that easy to leave behind.

"What about your estate?" she asked him. "And your work?"

"I can work from anywhere in the world. And my estate is not nearly as important to me as you are It's just a house, Kate. I see that now. My legacy lies with you; not with a building."

Kate smiled. They sat together for a while longer and then Ford eased the car onto the ferry as soon as the gate opened.

Once the ferry was in motion, both Ford and Kate gazed trustingly at each other as they breathed a sigh of relief. On the journey, they spoke about what they would do now and where they would go They had left the house and indeed the island so quickly in order to get away as fast as possible, but now the options of where they could go were limitless. Ford had enough money for them to move anywhere in the world once they were calm enough to put their heads together. Kate liked the idea of somewhere overseas and far away; a place where they could build their own house and start completely over together, a place with only one bedroom that they would share (at least, until they started having children and needed additional bedrooms).

It was nighttime when they got off the ferry. Ford made arrangements for a hotel. Thoughts of going on honeymoon thereafter soon crossed his mind. After all, this was something that he really should have done all along. Such was the influence of the house and the island on his tired and frightened mind at the time. For too long, he had been willing to accept living in fear of the angry spirit that haunted his own home. He could see that now. Kate had helped him. Her boldness to ask questions and her refusal to accept things being swept under the carpet had ultimately freed them both.

Once settled in the hotel bed, Ford fell asleep against Kate's shoulder. Her nerves were still too frazzled for her to close her eyes. It concerned her that Isaac and the crow had seemed to vanish into thin air. She wondered about whether or not spirits were bound to the houses that they haunted. She'd never had any experience with the paranormal before so she had no idea how that sort of thing worked, but she imagined that it would be realistic to assume that Isaac and his awful bird had got what they wanted; his empty estate back.

Happy to leave Ford sleeping, Kate got up to get a glass of water and it wasn't long before she found herself looking out of the hotel window. She knew that sleep would come soon enough. She was exhausted and she knew that she could take comfort now in the fact that her husband would continue to share a bed with her. She felt closer to him than she had ever done before, especially after what they had been through together. She was beyond touched by all that her husband had put himself through in order to protect her, even though he had dared to try appeasing an angry spirit, and even though he had introduced her to such a dangerous situation. All that mattered now was that they were safe and had a promising future to look forward to.

The moon was gorgeous that night; it illuminated the nocturnal bustle of the city in the most enchanting way. As Kate scanned the beauty of the refreshing change of scenery, something just happened to catch her eye. She squinted to see what it was that was casting a silhouette so far up in the sky. When she saw that it wasn't a shadow at all, her breath stopped. There, perched on top of a street lamp, was the crow.

****

Lightning Source UK Ltd.
Milton Keynes UK
UKHW022021101221
395433UK00011B/1039